Wicked Woods

kailin gow

Wicked Woods

Wicked Woods
Published by THE EDGE
THE EDGE is an imprint of Sparklesoup LLC
Copyright © 2010 Kailin Gow

For information, please contact:

THE EDGE at Sparklesoup
P.O. Box 60834
Irvine, CA 92602
www.sparklesoup.com
First Edition.
Printed in the United States of America.

ISBN: 1597486310
ISBN: 978-1597486316

DEDICATION

For my awesome editors, cover artist, and theEDGEbooks.com team. Thank you for helping me make the story of Briony and the townspeople of Wicked, MA come alive.

Prologue

Briony Patterson was in bed, unable to sleep, fearing that simply closing her eyes would bring forth the monsters she thought lived in the dark. Except for the full moon shining through the window of her room, it was dark. Very dark. So dark Briony could barely see her fingers in front of her. Scary things happen in the dark. Bad things happen in the dark. As far as Briony could see, there was a lot of darkness in front of her, laid out in acres over acres of woodland.

Briony could not close her eyes into blissful sleep, for this was the same house her parents and little brother had stayed in before they vanished forever, leaving her an orphan, leaving her alone, except for Aunt Sophie, who owned this little bed and breakfast at the edge of the Wicked Woods.

Briony turned, trying to make herself more comfortable in the rickety antique bed. It was the wrong bed. Briony's bed was small, and comfortable, and hundreds of miles away. The Edge Inn was nice enough, but Briony still couldn't think of it as *her* room. Thinking that would be like admitting that she would never be going back, that her parents and little brother weren't waiting for her in her real home. Of course, they weren't, but that only made it worse.

This wasn't home, this old-fashioned little place in the town of Wicked, Massachusetts, even though her aunt was working hard to make it feel that way. It was too antiquated, with its exposed beams and its leaded windows, too isolated, and above all too *different* feeling. Had her brother had this room? No wonder Briony couldn't get to sleep.

She closed her eyes for a second. It was still hard to believe her entire family was gone. Missing. Vanished. Into the woods, never to be found…into the very woods staring at her right outside the windows of this seemingly cozy little guest room.

Although Aunt Sophie was kind enough to take her in after her parents and little brother's disappearance,

Wicked Woods

Briony knew Aunt Sophie didn't want her here to complicate her life. Aunt Sophie lost Uncle Pete in the same excursion into the woods that took away Briony's family. The last thing Aunt Sophie wanted in her life was probably a teenager.

But Aunt Sophie was the only family she had now, and Briony was Aunt Sophie's. Briony didn't want to be here, away from her home in Florida, away from her friends, away from the life she once had. Briony took a deep breath. Adjusting to this new life would be hard. She missed her old life, she missed her parents, and even her irritating little brother Jake, but it sure beat being homeless. She experienced being that for about one week after her family's disappearance, and her house was sold to pay bills she didn't know about. Briony found herself without a home for nearly a week, staying with friends, then a shelter…until Aunt Sophie could claim her as her legal relative and move her over to Wicked. Somehow, there was a paperwork mixed up, which Briony couldn't understand. Great Aunt Sophie and Uncle Pete had always been part of her family, but Briony had never understood her mother's connection with Aunt Sophie, besides Aunt Sophie being a distant relative.

Briony got up and went over to the full-length mirror in one corner. Her honey blonde hair was a mess from all the tossing and turning she had been doing, trying to get to sleep. Her blue eyes were just starting to take on that hollow look that came when you went without sleep too long, making her normally pretty features look older than their sixteen years.

Outside the window, something howled. Briony was used to Florida, where the only sounds at night were of cars, and horns and occasional sirens. Now though, she found herself living next to about a thousand acres of woodland, complete with mysterious howling creatures. She didn't even know if what was out there was a stray dog or a wolf deeper in the forest.

Briony moved over to the window, staring through the diamond pattern of the glass at the world outside. Even with the moon out, there wasn't much to see here on the very edge of town. It was so much darker out here at night than in the cities she was used to. It took some getting used to.

She should have been getting used to it last month, when her family came up to stay with Great Aunt Sophie and Uncle Pete. It hadn't sounded like much fun, even then.

Wicked Woods

Slogging around in the wilderness wasn't really for her. Thankfully, Briony's parents had agreed, and she had gone off to cheerleading camp instead. That had been so much better, right up to the point when the phone call came through to tell her that her mother, father, brother and uncle were gone, just like that.

Something moved in the darkness, out beyond the window. Briony forced herself not to jump. It was probably just a small animal or something. Except that when it came again, Briony couldn't see anything. Instead, all she could see were shadows, shifting as a deeper darkness on the edge of the trees around the inn. Oh yes, the Edge Inn, run on the edge of the forest by Sophie Edge and her husband. That seemed *so* funny now that there were *things* out there, didn't it?

Wrapping a thick robe over her nightclothes, Briony set off downstairs, knowing that there was no way that she would sleep yet. She had only gone to bed because Aunt Sophie had suggested that it might be good to get an early night, what with starting at Wicked's High School tomorrow. Well, that and she suspected that her great aunt probably needed some time alone. It couldn't be easy trying to be strong for Briony when Aunt Sophie had her own grief to deal with over the loss of Uncle Pete. Briony knew that her aunt would never show any hint of it around her, because that wasn't the kind of thing Aunt Sophie did.

Briony tiptoed downstairs, determined not to wake anyone, though with no guests currently at the inn, there was only Aunt Sophie to worry about. Briony found her asleep in the lounge. She lay in an armchair, wrapped in a robe so voluminous that it made her look vaguely like a yeti and snoring in tones that probably accounted for the lack of guests. Two fluffy pink slippers poked out of the end of the robe. Her graying hair was tied back. It made Aunt Sophie look older than usual, showing all of her fifty years.

Briony crept quietly past her to the lounge's television, turning it on with the volume barely audible. The local news was on, which was probably good. So little seemed to happen around Wicked that Briony would probably be asleep in seconds. Alright, so that was probably unfair. Even so, there didn't seem to be much in the local news beyond the usual round of minor events. There was a Fall Moon Festival coming up, and apparently it was due to be the biggest for years. The local high school football schedule was announced, and people were urged to support the team on their big days. There were a few more announcements about tryouts for local sports teams, but again, it was nothing that seemed important.

When that was done and the news gave over to the weather, Briony decided that it was probably time to get back to bed. As quietly as she could, she switched off the TV and started to tiptoe back past her aunt, who was still snoring loud enough to wake the dead. Briony didn't want to disturb her.

She had made it almost as far as the stairs when the doorbell rang. Briony didn't bother looking around for a clock. She already knew that it was far too late for people to be showing up looking for a room. On the other hand, though, it wasn't like there were any guests at the moment, and Aunt Sophie would probably be glad for the extra business.

"I'm coming," Briony muttered under her breath as the doorbell rang again. "Can you not hold on one minute?"

Briony hurried for the door, but she was not as quick as her great aunt. In the time it took Briony to cross the hallway, Aunt Sophie managed to wake up, leave her chair, and place herself firmly between Briony and the door. Briony found herself smiling at the thought of the sight Aunt Sophie probably presented as she opened it in that huge, furry robe of hers.

She was certainly a contrast to the couple waiting on the doorstep. They were so glamorous that they could have passed for Hollywood celebrities, though possibly ones from the nineteen-forties, given the way they dressed. The man had slicked back blond hair, a suit that was complete with waistcoat and pocket-watch, and even old-fashioned spats on his shoes. The woman was resplendent in a red dress that matched her lipstick, while her hair fell loose in blond waves. Both of them seemed very pale to Briony, who was used to people who got out in the Florida sun. Also, there seemed to be something slightly odd about their eyes. Maybe they were wearing colored contact lenses?

"What is it you want?" Aunt Sophie asked. Her voice wasn't friendly. She probably didn't like having to answer the door dressed as she was in the middle of the night.

The man smiled. His voice, when it came, seemed a touch too smooth. "We're sorry to call on you so late, ma'am, but we were just at a party. We have been driving back through the woods, but it occurred to us that we didn't really want to drive all night. We were hoping that you might still have some rooms."

The woman clung to his arm as he said this. She directed a smile at Briony.

"Oh, look, Philip. Isn't she sweet?"

Briony was a little surprised when Aunt Sophie edged a little further in front of her, though not as surprised as at what she said next.

"I think it's time you left. We don't have any rooms. Try someplace else."

"That isn't very friendly," the woman said, frowning.

"Like I said, try someplace else."

Something about the couple changed then. They were still smiling, but to Briony, those smiles looked a lot more predatory. The way their canine teeth suddenly looked a lot longer probably had something to do with it. They started to take a step forward.

So fast that Briony barely saw it, Aunt Sophie reached into her robe and drew out two objects. One was a glass vial, which she waved as though the contents were dangerous. The other was, of all things, a large silver crucifix. It looked to Briony like a moment from some bad horror movie, except that the visitors *did* look scared, and they *did* reel back from the sight of the cross.

They hissed like angry cats, but didn't come any closer. Aunt Sophie uncorked the vial in her hand, and they scrambled backwards as if they were in a film that was being rewinded. They turned, running into the nearby woods and vanishing from sight in the darkness.

Briony stood there staring where the couple had been a few minutes ago, her brain and body paralyzed to the reality of what she had witnessed with her own eyes. It couldn't be true. They only exist in movies, books, and folklore. She bit her lips. She could scream, or faint, or try running up to her room and barricading the door, but those all struck her as stupid things to do. Instead she settled for a nervous grin, trying to remain calm for Aunt Sophie.

"Um... were those... vampires?" She said it in the tone of someone fully expecting, and frankly rather hoping, that her great aunt would tell her not to be so silly.

Instead, Aunt Sophie nodded as she shut the door. "They were." She paused and then said with a wry smile. "Welcome to Wicked, Briony."

"And that's the welcoming committee, is it?" Briony was starting to feel a little light-headed.

"Oh, they're nothing. Amateurs who can't get the hang of the fact that you don't wander around wearing evening dress if you want to prey on people. It's the ones that look just like you or me that are the problem. Well, them and a few... other things. You get all kinds in Wicked."

They certainly did. Briony considered fainting, but thought better of it. Somehow with Aunt Sophie around, Briony felt she needed to hold herself together. Aunt Sophie wasn't the crying or fainting type, and for some reason, Briony wanted her to see she can be strong, too.

"Um... what's in the vial?"

"Holy water, obviously. I bless up a big batch now and then. I'll tell you, Briony, my life got a lot easier the day it became possible to be ordained a minister over the Internet. Also, it's kind of useful when we have couples come through looking to get married."

"Yes," Briony said, "it would be." Briony kept her voice calm, making sure her eyes didn't widen in surprise. What the heck was Aunt Sophie? Certainly Aunt Sophie had a double life the family didn't know of...blessing a batch of holy water?

Aunt Sophie put an arm around Briony's shoulders. The bottle of holy water pressed up against Briony's back, so it wasn't entirely comforting.

Vampires? Howling things outside her window? A vast woodland just steps away from this inn...where her entire family disappeared? Anyone with some kind of sanity would have high-tailed it out of the same place where your family disappeared, right? No, not Aunt Sophie. Briony couldn't hold her question back any further. "Why does anyone stay in a place like this?" she suddenly blurted.

Aunt Sophie just smiled. "I can see that this has been a bit of a shock for you, but you'll feel better after a good night's sleep. C'mon, back to bed. You have school in the morning and you'll want to make a good impression."

Briony let herself be shepherded back upstairs to her new room. With everything that had just happened though, sleep proved even more elusive than ever.

Wicked Woods
Chapter 1

As first impressions went, Briony suspected that she had made better ones. The lack of sleep didn't help. Staying up until four in the morning because you were still trying to process the fact that there were *vampires* in the world. And that they can just come up to you, knock on your door, and smile charmingly at you like normal people was enough of a shock to keep Briony scrambling around in her room for anything she thought would help keep them away from her. She didn't let on to Aunt Sophie how frightened she was of this newfound knowledge, especially the way Aunt Sophie acted like it was an everyday thing. This everyday thing was what worried Briony. She did not sleep a wink, which was not a good way to prepare for your first day at a new school.

Then there was the way she was dressed. The simple dark dress and patterned sweater were ordinary enough, but most people in her class didn't wear makeshift cross around their necks consisting of two carefully sharpened pencils stuck together with packing tape. Briony had hidden the cross necklace under her dress, hoping no one would see it. She knew it was stupid-looking, but it was all she could find in her room. She figured, if there were vampires coming after her like last night, at least she had something that might work. She didn't know much about vampires, except what she saw in the movies. She could've kick herself for not paying more attention. What were vampires afraid of? Silver?

Briony looked down at her wrist. It was a last minute thing, but after raiding Aunt Sophie's kitchen this morning for anything silver, she found some spoons, which she bent into a kind of bracelet. Not exactly what she would've worn to school on her first day, but it made her feel a little safer.

And then there was the effect of the smell to consider. It was amazing how much garlic you could sneak onto your breakfast if you tried, and Briony had certainly tried. The end result was breath that might or might not have stopped a vampire from getting near to her, but which was certainly stopping everything and everyone else.

The upshot of all this was a series of stares as she entered her classes, followed by the kind of whispering that never boded well. Occasionally, Briony heard words like "freak" and "weirdo" floating out from little cliques of girls, while the boys who might have spent time staring at her or trying to talk to her at her old school avoided her completely here.

Frankly, Briony had bigger things to worry about, and if anything, that was the one good thing about the day. She was so busy worrying over and looking out for vampires that there wasn't really any time to worry about the usual "am I understanding anything in class?" or "do the popular girls like me?" questions.

The thing that struck Briony as strange was that everybody else wasn't as freaked out about living in Wicked as she was. Didn't they know that they lived in a town containing vampires? That the Wicked Woods in Wicked was home to vampires, werewolves, ghouls, and anything supernatural?

As the day wore on, it occurred to Briony that no, they probably *didn't* know. How could they? If people in one town knew that vampires were real, then people everywhere would know. It wasn't the kind of thing you could keep to just one place. Someone would phone their cousin in the next town, or post footage on the Internet, or even just stick up a big sign at the edge of town saying, "Incidentally, there are vampires here." Somehow, the news would get out, wouldn't it?

Well, there had certainly been nothing about it in Briony's introductions to her classes, though to be fair, she had been so sleepy at the time that a teacher could easily have said, "Class, this is Briony, she's new, so be sure to tell her all about avoiding the undead," and she might not have noticed. Still, nobody had come up to her to give her any tips along the lines of "be sure to run if you see any bats." Of course, practically nobody had come up to her at all, and it was lunchtime now. Maybe things would change in the school cafeteria, though Briony wasn't particularly hopeful.

It was nice to see that, in some respects, schools were the same everywhere. The cafeteria was a large space made smaller by the number of tables stuffed into it, and one look at some of the students' faces told her that the food was going to be only just the right side of inedible. Briony grabbed a tray, and ended up with something generously described as spaghetti bolognaise. They ignored her request for extra garlic.

Wicked Woods

Briony looked around for somewhere to sit, and found that things were familiar in another respect too. The school's inhabitants clustered in little clumps and cliques that split along lines Briony could pick out easily. The jocks from the football team occupied a couple of tables shoved together, not far from a group of pretty girls who had to be cheerleaders. A set of geeky-looking kids sat further off, apparently arguing about some computer game Briony had never heard of. A couple of girls with flute cases bolted their food so that they could get to some kind of band practice.

There were some Goths in one corner. Briony avoided them instinctively. After all, in a place like this, what kind of person *wanted* to dress like a wannabe member of the walking dead? Briony found herself thinking of her great aunt's warning that the dangerous ones were the ones where you couldn't tell, but she suspected that in at least some cases you definitely *could*.

Inevitably, Briony found herself gravitating towards the group that looked like they were cheerleaders. It was where she fit in, after all. At her old school, she would have been sitting in the middle of a group like that, easily the prettiest girl in her class, with plenty of friends around her.

She wouldn't have been standing around, looking for the spot where she fit in, because she would already have known.

Briony made it to the edge of the little group before one of them detached herself from the conversation to intercept her. She was dark-haired, blue-eyed, and expensively dressed. Just her shoes would have cost as much as Briony's entire outfit, even if Briony hadn't been looking quite so bedraggled from lack of sleep. Just from the way the other girls looked at the rich girl, Briony could tell that she was in charge. It was important at times like these to be confident and outgoing, even if you mostly felt tired. Briony did her best.

"Hi, I'm Briony."

"Oh, how sweet, the weird new girl wants to sit with us." It was not a promising beginning. "Well, I'm Pepper Freeman."

She said it like she expected that Briony would have heard of her already. Briony looked around at the rest of the group. They seemed to be content to watch the unfolding show.

"You're must be... let's see... head cheerleader? You look the type." It wasn't the most diplomatic way of putting it, but then, Briony was a bit too tired for that kind of thing.

"Of course I'm head cheerleader. And if we're talking about *types*, what's yours?" she got hold of Briony's pencil cross, which had slipped out from under her dress and was in plain view. "Some kind of low budget Goth, maybe? Perhaps a weird hybrid of Goth and Nerd. Not exactly the most *elegant* of fashion statements, is it?"

"Yeah," said someone in the back, obviously Pepper's groupie. Briony considered a comment on the other girl's jewelry. It was certainly easy to spot. What kind of person wore what looked like genuine diamond earrings to school? Someone, or more likely her father's credit card, had been very generous.

"Look," Briony said, "I don't want trouble, I just want to eat my lunch."

"Then go somewhere and eat it, weird girl." Pepper held her nose. "Presumably, you'll fit in somewhere people can't smell that garlic breath."

That got a laugh from the other girls. Of course it did. When your official head mean girl gave you the signal that you should be laughing at someone, you laughed at them, because the alternative was finding yourself as her next target. Briony knew how it worked. She was the Pepper Freeman at her old school, but she was never that mean...was she? Hopefully not. That didn't make her feel any better as the laugh rolled out over her, though.

If she hadn't been feeling so tired, she might have been able to come up with some witty comeback that would have put Pepper Freeman in her place. If she hadn't had enough garlic in her to stun passers-by, she would certainly have been able to at least reach out to them. It wouldn't have taken much. It never did. As it was though, Briony found herself beating a hasty retreat to eat her lunch on her own, in that corner of the cafeteria that seemed to be reserved for loners and misfits. She didn't even try fitting in with one of the other groups. There didn't seem to be much point.

After lunch, she was subjected to physics and English. Things didn't get much better. Briony did her best, but her concentration waned when faced with the onslaught of sleep deprivation. And news of her brief conversation with the head cheerleader had obviously gotten round. Girls who thought that they fit in with that clique, or at least that they should, didn't bother hiding their smirks as they looked at Briony. More than a few made their own comments about garlic, just quietly enough that the teacher didn't hear.

Briony had the worst school day in her life. She couldn't just rise above it all, because the comments and the looks kept coming. She couldn't react either, because the moment she opened her mouth to do so, a teacher would give her a stern "you don't want to get into trouble on your first day" look. The only thing she could really do was sit there and try not to let any of her frustration show.

Briony was so grateful for the final bell that she practically sighed with relief. She wanted to run straight to her great aunt's car, but she didn't. Briony forced herself to walk slowly and confidently. The more scared she looked, the more people would start to think of her as an easy victim. That would only make things worse. You couldn't let fear control you.

Of course, Briony realized she had been doing exactly that all day. All that stuff with the garlic had just been crazy. And not being able to calm down enough to sleep was about the worst move she could have made. Fear, specifically the fear of vampires, had ended up making her a social misfit. At this rate, she would be lucky if her classmates ever accepted her. She shook her head, removing her improvised cross and vowing to find a breath mint at the first opportunity. So vampires were real, so what? She still had to go to school. She still had to find a way to fit in. If she let fear rule her, Briony knew that she might never have a social life again.

Her decision made, Briony felt a lot happier. Things would be better tomorrow. Almost certainly. Even so, she was immensely happy when she finally slid into the passenger seat of the battered old Ford Aunt Sophie drove. Her great aunt looked Briony over with an expression that said she had a pretty good idea of exactly how Briony's day had gone. Even so, she smiled.

"Rough day, darling? Well, I thought, this being your first day and all, I should take you out to celebrate anyway. Maybe it will make you feel better."

Briony was too tired to answer as Aunt Sophie put the car in gear and set off. Wherever they were going, it had to be better than this.

Chapter 2

Aunt Sophie's treat turned out to be a visit to a diner called George's, which was a tidy, neat little place close to the center of Wicked. Aunt Sophie led Briony inside, and Briony found herself staring at some of the photos on the wall, which seemed to encompass every famous, nearly famous, and not at all famous person who had visited the town in the last century or so.

"Ignore them," Aunt Sophie said, following Briony's gaze. "George got them at a garage sale so that he could give this place a sense of history. He actually opened it fifteen years ago. I know. I was there."

"You were indeed." A good-looking man in his early fifties stepped out from what was probably a kitchen to greet them. His greying hair was cut so short that Briony just *knew* he had been in the military at some point, and his physique seemed to bear it out. This was not someone who had let himself slow down as he aged. "Hello, Sophie. How's the most beautiful woman in Wicked?"

Briony watched her great aunt roll her eyes. "Briony, I would like you to meet my friend George. Do your best to ignore him. I only put up with him because he also happens to make some of the best food in town."

The man grinned. "Why, is that a compliment? Who would have thought it? Now, what can I get the two of you today?"

They had burgers and milkshakes, sitting at the counter to eat them. Both were indeed delicious, though Briony found herself having to deal with the sight of her aunt attacking her burger with a level of enthusiasm that Briony suspected you probably weren't supposed to see in elegant older ladies.

While they ate, George wandered off to serve other customers, and there were certainly plenty of those. A red-headed waitress in her twenties, whom Aunt Sophie greeted as Jill, handled most of them, but there always seemed to be more. Apparently, news about the quality of the food had spread. Even so, George kept coming back to chat with the pair of them, asking polite questions of Briony, but mostly keeping up the kind of running argument with Aunt Sophie that you generally only got between people who had been friends for years. Finally though, he got around to asking the one question Briony had kind of been hoping to avoid.

"So, how were things on your first day at the school?"

Briony thought about lying, just to be polite, but her great aunt was watching her too, and Aunt Sophie had always been able to tell when she wasn't telling the truth.

"It was," she declared at last, "the single worst day of my life, socially, at least."

"Oh?" George had acquired a milkshake glass, which he started polishing. Briony wasn't sure if it really needed cleaning, or if he had just decided that it was the kind of thing people should do while they were listening to other people's troubles. "What happened?"

"Um…" Briony wasn't sure how an explanation involving vampires would go until Aunt Sophie patted her on the arm.

"It's all right, Briony. George knows as much about these things as I do. Or he likes to think he does, at least."

"This from the woman who has been working on the idea of ecumenical holy water?"

"It *might* work."

Briony did her best to explain, if only to cut off the beginnings of the banter. She spent much of the explanation fighting the urge to blush with embarrassment. Now that she came to explain them to someone else, the things she had done today did indeed seem more than a little stupid. She explained about the events of the previous night, keeping her voice low until Aunt Sophie pointed out that no one else would believe what they heard, even if they did overhear something they shouldn't.

After that, Briony talked normally, explaining about the garlic and the improvised crucifix, the falling asleep in class and the name-calling. When she got to the part with the head cheerleader, George raised an eyebrow.

"This would be Pepper Freeman? She comes in here sometimes. Always looking round to make sure someone is watching her. My guess is that she didn't like the potential competition."

"Competition?" Briony said. "I had garlic breath."

George shrugged. "Well, whatever. I hope you won't let it put you off, anyway."

"Yes, Briony," Aunt Sophie put in. "You mustn't let one bad day ruin your academic career."

Wicked Woods

Briony shook her head. She didn't have any plans to let that happen. "I'll be fine. I just need to find some ways of making sure I don't get bitten by vampires that don't include me looking like a total idiot to the rest of the school."

"There's worse than that out..." George began. Aunt Sophie stopped him with a look. "What?"

"My niece barely slept last night, and you want to tell her horror stories about your past?"

Briony shook her head. "I don't mind, Aunt Sophie. I think I'm probably going to be tired enough to sleep tonight no matter what happens. Besides, it can't be any worse than last night."

Aunt Sophie gave her a long look. "Oh, how I wish that were true, child. Still, we probably *should* come up with some ideas that don't leave you a social outcast. Ah, I remember my first day at school. This *horrid* boy insisted on following me around, making fun of the way I had my hair."

"What happened?" Briony asked. "What did you do about him?"

"Oh, things eventually settled down with Peter once I married him. Of course, that's not much of a help to you. George, should we take this into your office?"

The diner owner nodded. "Jill, are you okay to take care of things out here for a few minutes?"

"Sure," the waitress said, "just remember that it's not long till I get off for the afternoon. I have to pick up Sarah from the crèche."

George nodded, leading the way back behind the counter and into a small office, kept with the kind of neatness that matched his haircut. Not a scrap of paper looked to be out of place on the desk off to one side, while two chairs were aligned perfectly with it. A couple of framed certificates indicated prizes the restaurant had won for the quality of its food.

Only a couple of points didn't really fit in. The wooden panels that lined the room looked like they'd been added as an afterthought. More oddly, a stuffed moose's head sat on the wall opposite the desk, gazing down on events with what Briony thought was a rather mournful expression.

"Shut the door," George instructed, and Briony did so. Aunt Sophie smiled the secret smile of someone who knew what was coming next, and who was looking forward to seeing the expression on her niece's face when it did.

George reached up to the moose, twisting one antler. There was a click, a whir, and a couple of the panels on the wall slid back to reveal a high tech cubby hole filled with enough weapons to arm most of the town. There were crossbows with silver quarrels. There were stakes. There were silver-bladed knives and even a few swords. Other objects caught Briony's eye. A neat stack of bibles sat next to a collection of silver crosses, while jars of herbs stood labelled off to one side.

On the backs of the panels that had swung back, there were maps and hand-drawn diagrams. One purported to show the weaknesses of werewolves, with arrows pointing to the eyes, the throat, the heart, and other easy to hurt spots. There weren't many. A map detailed the area around Wicked, pointing out paths through the woods, the locations of caches of weapons and supplies, the known hunting grounds of supernatural creatures, and other items of interest.

To Briony, it was all interesting. Interesting, and more than a little frightening.

"You have all this in here and nobody knows about it? People don't know about the vampires?"

"Some do," Aunt Sophie told her. "George's cook and pot washer both know, and so does Jill, whom you saw outside. Peter did, obviously, and there are a few others."

"All the members of the Wicked Woods Preservation Society, for example," George said. "It's a very important society around here, but people outside of the society don't get we are more interested in preserving the people of Wicked and the surrounding woods than its historic buildings."

"They just don't want to face up to what's around them," Aunt Sophie said. She sounded quite dismissive. "But then, I suppose it can be dangerous if you do."

It's why all the members carry these." George picked up one of the crucifixes. It seemed a little bulky for its size as Briony held it.

"There's more to this than meets the eye, isn't there?" she guessed. George and her great aunt gave her pleased looks.

"The cross is silver," Aunt Sophie explained, "so that it's useful against werewolves. The center is hollow, containing a vial of holy water which you can uncap."

Wicked Woods

George flipped open the top. "There's also vervain below the vial," he explained. "That makes it harder for anything to control your mind. Harder, but not impossible. And there's one last feature that is especially useful." He pressed something on the cross, and the end extended by several inches. It looked sharp. "A stake. More than long enough to reach the heart."

Briony looked at the device for several seconds before she spoke. "I guess that's a lot better than improvising something out of pencils."

"It is," Aunt Sophie said, taking the pendant from George and hanging it on a silver chain. When she was done, it looked like nothing more than a slightly bulky crucifix once again. "Which is why I would like you to wear it, Briony."

Briony stood still while her great aunt hung it around her neck, letting it fall out of sight under Briony's sweater. The metal lay cool against her skin. Somehow, just wearing it made her feel a lot safer.

"There," Aunt Sophie said. "That should keep you a lot safer than any garlic would, and you'll probably be a lot more popular too. For future reference, most vampires don't care one way or the other about garlic. Not everything you've heard about them will be correct."

"Then what is?" Briony asked. "I mean, if one comes at me, how do I kill it?"

"Would you listen to her?" George said, with a widening grin. "Already, she's wondering how to kill them. You have picked well here, Sophie."

"Picked me for what?" Briony asked. The other two ignored her.

Aunt Sophie nodded. "I know. The girl is a natural. But then, it's in her blood."

"Picked me for *what*?" Briony insisted.

Her great aunt shrugged. "Why, to be my replacement as a vampire hunter, of course, Briony. It's what we do, after all."

Chapter 3

Aunt Sophie caught the slightly shocked expression on Briony's face, because she took her by the arm.

"Perhaps I should explain. Come and sit down, Briony."

Briony did as her great aunt had asked her, taking the chair on the far side of George's desk. The diner owner, meanwhile, twisted the moose's horn again, and the secret compartment in his office closed up so completely that Briony could hardly believe it had been there at all.

"I've got to go out and take over for Jill," George said. He nodded to Briony. "I'm sure that everything will work out. Just listen to what Sophie has to say."

Briony nodded back, even though she didn't feel very confident. Aunt Sophie *really* wanted her to hunt vampires? It was only once George had gone that the older woman started to talk.

"Wicked is a very old town, at least by the standards of this country. It has been here since a few years after the first settlers arrived on the Mayflower…the very first settlers. It started life as… I suppose you could call it a kind of resort. It's a place where people came when they were sick of working in other towns, or needed to be closer to the wilderness. There weren't many at first, but there were enough."

"Enough for what?" Briony asked, mostly because she suspected that was what Aunt Sophie wanted her to ask. This sounded a lot like the kind of conversation where the adult involved had worked out her half of it in advance.

"Enough for vampires to take an interest in them." Aunt Sophie shook her head. "People didn't see it at first, of course. People would go missing, and it would be explained away by bears, or wolves, or even outlaws. After all, who would think that there might be vampires out there?"

Briony nodded. She didn't have any difficulties with the idea herself, what with having seen a pair of the creatures, but it was easy to understand that people wouldn't want to believe in them. Aunt Sophie kept going.

Wicked Woods

"For some reason, over the years this little town has become quite a hot spot for supernatural creatures of all sorts. Vampires, werewolves, if you can name it, it has probably tried to eat assorted members of the local population at some point. Maybe it's because this town is so close to somewhere wild, where they can get lost in the wilderness. Maybe it's something different about the town." Aunt Sophie looked wistful for a moment. "Peter always thought that there might be something in the water, making things go crazy around here. Spent hours testing local creeks and springs. Silly man."

Briony could hear the note of regret there. She had to ask. "So Uncle Peter knew all about vampires?"

"Oh, absolutely. He and I found out together, while we were still at school. We both found hunters willing to teach us, and we ended up killing the creatures together for years. After a while, it gets so that you know someone so well, it's almost like there aren't two of you fighting anymore. It's just one of you that happens to have four arms and four legs." Aunt Sophie thought for a moment.

Briony shook her head. "Sorry. It's just all a bit…"

"Insane?"

Briony nodded. Her great aunt reached out to pat her hand. "I know, dear. The first time I heard it, I thought it was utter madness, but *someone* has to keep these things in check."

Briony bit nervously at her lip. "You make it sound like killing vampires is organized. Like it's some big secret society, or something."

"It isn't quite on that scale," Aunt Sophie said, "but yes, we are organized. We have been almost from the beginning. People who slay vampires have existed in almost every country for thousands of years, doing their best to keep people safe. Most of the time, they are simply very ordinary people who happen to have a lot of training and the right equipment. Just knowing about vampires is almost half the battle." She paused. "Of course, the other half is stopping the things from killing you long enough to stake them, but you can't have everything."

Briony tried to imagine it, but there is only so much you can imagine on only a couple of hours sleep. A nearly endless war against supernatural predators who saw the human race as nothing more than a mobile buffet didn't seem to be one of them. Another thing she was having a hard time imagining was Aunt Sophie doing battle with the forces of darkness.

"Um... Aunt Sophie? Don't take this the wrong way, but you don't exactly *look* like a vampire slayer."

Her great aunt cocked her head to one side. "And what does one of those look like, Briony? Some young woman in too much leather, wearing dozens of knives? Some hulking man weighed down by so much weaponry that he'll fall over backwards if you push him hard enough?"

"Um..." Briony hadn't given much thought to it. She suspected that most people didn't. If she did have to describe the kind of person who hunted vampires though, she was certain of one thing. It *wouldn't* be the kind of person who wore pink fluffy slippers at night and fell asleep in front of the television.

"Let's try this another way, shall we?" Aunt Sophie suggested. "In a fair fight with a supernatural creature that is faster, stronger, and generally deadlier than the average human, how much use do you think it would be to be some pumped up bodybuilder?"

When she put it like that, it was obvious what answer Aunt Sophie wanted. "Not much," Briony said.

"Exactly. So we don't fight fair. We kill them before they have a chance to turn it into a fight. We take them by surprise." She paused, looking Briony up and down. "Often, the people best placed to do that are the ones who don't look that dangerous. Frail old ladies like myself, for example."

Briony couldn't help laughing at that. "Frail?"

Aunt Sophie smiled. "All right, maybe not that frail. And I note that you didn't say anything about the old part, young lady. But the point remains. I don't *look* dangerous, so I can get close enough to kill them. And so could you."

There was the heart of it. Aunt Sophie wanted to take Briony and have her kill things that until yesterday she hadn't known existed. That had kept her awake last night just thinking of them. More than that, she wanted to send Briony out against things that she had just as good as said could kill her in any kind of fight.

"So why are you doing this?" Briony asked. "Why are you trying to recruit me to do this?"

"You mean aside from the fact that someone has to protect people?" Aunt Sophie asked. Briony could see the sympathy there. She clearly knew how much she was asking. "Well, I said before that this wasn't some big secret society, but we're still organized enough to have rules. One is that a vampire hunter has to train at least one successor before he or she can retire. I am, as you so rightly pointed out, getting a bit old for this."

Briony nodded. She could kind of understand that. "Ok, that makes sense. I mean, there must be a lot to teach people. Vampire slaying probably isn't the kind of thing you can pick up by trial and error."

Aunt Sophie shook her head. "It's the 'error' part that is the difficulty there. It isn't the kind of thing where you get many second chances. Yes, there's a lot to learn."

"Like what?"

Aunt Sophie raised her hands, ticking things off on her fingers. "Hand to hand combat, weapons, basic anatomy-you'd be *amazed* at how many people don't know where the heart is, and it's always embarrassing if you stake anywhere else-silent movement, surviving in the forest, and a dozen other things besides. And that's just with vampires. There are so many types of creature to learn about, none of them particularly nice."

Briony tried not to think about that, but it wasn't exactly easy. Besides, her great aunt seemed to be promising her nothing more than a great deal of training, with the near certainty of eventually being killed by a vampire as a reward for it. She tried to think of a way to put it.

"Aunt Sophie, I know all this is important, and I can see why you might need to train a successor, but-"

"Why you?"

Briony nodded, and her great aunt shrugged.

"I think you have the right qualities to be an exceptional vampire hunter. You're athletic, but not dangerous looking. You're smarter than you let on, and pretty enough that a lot of the things will underestimate you. You're tenacious, but still compassionate. And of course, you have as much reason as anyone to hate the things."

Briony went still. She licked her lips. "Are you saying that my parents were..." she couldn't say it.

Aunt Sophie squeezed her hand. "None of us can know for certain, but when people go missing in *these* woods, there are only a few options when it comes to what has happened."

Briony couldn't help thinking about it. About vampires like the ones that had come to the door falling on her parents and drinking their blood. About them killing her brother. Even though she tried to push the images away, they still came back. Something rose in her then, angry, but not hot with anger. If anything, it felt cold. Cold, and violent, and eager for revenge.

"I'll do it," she said, her hands clenching. "When do we start?"

Aunt Sophie shook her head. "Not yet. That's one of the big things that you'll have to learn. All this has to fit in with a normal life."

"*Normal?*"

"Well, as normal as life can get while you're looking around for the undead. But I think we should at least get you settled into your school properly before we start thinking about things like this."

"But I want to start now."

Her great aunt shook her head, and Briony felt the first tears. She'd hardly cried since learning of her family's disappearance, but she cried now. Aunt Sophie held her, whispering meaningless things that barely registered as proper words. Somewhere along the line, Briony looked up enough to see that her great aunt was crying too. Was it for Uncle Peter, just as lost to Aunt Sophie as Briony's parents and brother were to her? Or was it at the thought of what she was about to turn Briony into?

"Shh, Briony. I shouldn't have told you all of this so soon after everything else that happened. If those fools hadn't come to the door like they did, I wouldn't have had to. For now, just concentrate on being a normal teenager. So long as you have your pendant with you, you should be safe enough."

Briony bit back the urge to smile bitterly. She was in a town full of vampires, about to be trained up into a vampire slayer by her great aunt, and have already convinced the rest of her school that she was a freak. Normal, Briony suspected, was no longer an option.

Chapter 4

The next morning came, and Briony met it feeling a lot more refreshed. With more knowledge of the dangers that were out there, she found that she wasn't nearly so worried. Of course, it helped that she also had some protection that might work, in the form of the cross her great aunt had given her.

The only question now was how things might go at school. After all, first impressions could do a lot of damage, and Briony had already made hers. Was it too late to change people's opinions of her? Would she be stuck as the loner girl who stank of garlic?

Briony was not going to let her disastrous first day at Wicked High dictate the rest of her high school career. She shook her head. As frighten she is about vampires, she now had to put it behind her. Aunt Sophie needed her. She was now part of Aunt Sophie's world, and that meant she had to get used to fighting vampires and whatever was out in the Wicked Woods. Didn't Aunt Sophie said someone's got to protect the people in Wicked? If there were more people like Aunt Sophie protecting people, then Briony's family would not have disappeared. Aunt Sophie needed her as her replacement. Wicked needed her.

Briony clamped her mouth into a determined grin and picked out her best jeans and a light pink top. As bad as her first day at school had been, she was going to grin and bear it. She brushed her silky hair until it was shiny and smooth, applied light makeup, and checked her appearance before she left the house. She was also careful to make sure that her cross pendant was still in place around her neck. Just because she felt a little safer now didn't mean that she was going to take chances.

She also felt a little better prepared for her classes now that she knew what they were going to be doing. With her mind not quite so firmly on vampires, Briony had been able to concentrate enough to do the reading required for the day's lessons. Hopefully, it would get her through. At least she wouldn't fall asleep this time.

Even so, when she arrived at school, Briony found herself taking a deep breath before she stepped through the door. She stopped herself. All she had to do was be confident. Briony did her best. She smiled and greeted the few people whose names she remembered. She walked down the corridors like she knew exactly what she was supposed to be doing, though she did have to pause a couple of times to ask the way to her first class.

"Oh, we're going that way," one of a pair of pretty, dark-haired girls said. Briony recognized them from the cafeteria the previous day. They'd laughed just as hard as anyone else at her. "We'll show you, if you like. I'm Tracey. This is Claire."

"Hi!" Claire said, or at least exclaimed. Briony had the feeling that she was going to be one of those people who had to exclaim things, mostly because the world was too exciting to merely say them. "You must be new!"

Briony considered pointing out that she had been just as new yesterday, but she didn't want to draw attention to yesterday if she could help it. Instead, she let Claire babble as they made their way to class, noticing that when people stared at her today, it was only to wonder who the pretty new girl was, not to point out the weirdo.

It was like she hadn't been there yesterday. People saw her, and they could hardly connect the image with what they'd seen of Briony before, so they ignored that part. The boys from the football team shot her admiring glances, while those friends of Claire and Tracey they passed nodded to her and welcomed her to the school.

Briony suspected that being with the other two helped there. It was like being accepted by a couple of the school's more popular girls was some kind of test, and having passed it, everyone else decided that she had to be all right. It probably wasn't the fairest way for things to work, but at that moment, Briony was prepared to accept it if it meant that people wouldn't make hurtful comments about her.

The first class was History, which Briony always enjoyed, and getting a few answers right proved to be another way of getting some attention from her classmates. Now, she wasn't just the pretty new girl, she qualified as smart too. The only slightly awkward part was that Briony spent a lot of the class wondering if any of what they were being taught was true. After all, if the teacher could get through the whole thing without mentioning vampires once, wasn't that proof that they weren't exactly being told the whole story?

That question gnawed at Briony a little as the morning classes continued. How much did supernatural things do in the world? How much got hidden? It wasn't easy learning things like biology when you already knew that there were things out there that didn't abide by rules as people knew them.

Even so, by the time lunch came around, Briony was feeling a lot happier than she had the day before. So far, things had gone without incident. Nothing had tried to eat her. No one had been mean. If anything, people had been kind. That kindness continued in the lunch hall, where Claire and Tracey invited Briony to sit with them. Briony took up the offer, and soon found herself sitting at the center of a cluster of the other girls' friends, talking about what life had been like back in Florida. Briony did her best to answer, though she steered things away from any mention of her family.

People drifted in and out of the group, but two boys named Bill and Ross were constants. Briony got the feeling that they liked Claire and Tracey, and were angling for dates. She had more sense than to get in the way. Besides, neither boy was really her type. Both had the bulky look of regular football players, along with nearly identical short haircuts and a tendency to finish each other's sentences. Briony wasn't sure if she could ever be that into someone who couldn't at least pretend to think for himself. Still, they seemed nice enough.

That was one good point about all of this. Briony could feel the press of the cross under her top, but no one around her seemed to be reacting to either it or the silver. It was a lot easier to relax when you were fairly sure that no one nearby was a vampire or a werewolf. Gradually, the conversation drifted onto topics other than Briony, for which she was actually a little grateful. There was only so long you could talk about yourself without feeling self-conscious or coming across as self-centered.

Besides, after a couple of days that had featured the weird, the outlandish, and the simply inhuman, Briony was grateful for the chance to talk about things as simple as boys, music, the chances of the football team winning (quite good), and the odds of Claire passing the math test they had coming up (not so great). Briony did her best to keep up, though in some ways it was like tuning into a soap opera where you didn't know any of the characters. Some things were easy to guess at, because the same kinds of things seemed to happen in most places, but at other times, Briony just had to smile, nod, and hope that it would all make some kind of sense once she knew who the people involved were.

Briony should probably have guessed that at some point, Pepper would show up. It was, after all, *her* clique of friends. Besides, she couldn't let the new girl gain admittance to it without at least putting in an appearance. She showed up about half way through lunch, still in a uniform that suggested she had been putting in some last minute practice before the big game.

She strode over with the confident gait of someone expecting her usual warm reception. When she didn't get quite the enthusiasm she had been hoping for, Pepper glared at Briony.

"Why, if it isn't garlic girl. What are *you* doing here?"

"Oh, leave her alone, Pepper," Tracey said, "she's okay."

When the others agreed, Briony felt her heart lift. Could it really be so easy to sort these things out? Certainly, Pepper seemed to let Briony's presence go without further comment for a while, as the conversation kept going on the same convoluted topics.

Eventually though, it somehow got back around to Briony. Pepper wanted to know all about her, and unlike when the others had been asking, her questions had barbs. The really annoying thing was that she managed to do it without ever sounding anything other than sympathetic.

"It must be really hard, having to move here, Briony. I heard that this is where your family went missing. That must be *so* hard."

Briony managed to mumble something that sounded vaguely like a response.

"I mean, if *my* family went missing, I would be completely broken up. You must be really strong to be coping so well."

"My Aunt Sophie has been great," Briony managed. She could feel sadness rising in her, and anger with it. If someone like Claire had made comments like this, Briony might have accepted it as just rather thoughtless. From Pepper though, it was obvious that everything Briony was struggling not to feel was *exactly* what she wanted.

"Your aunt? Oh yes…" Pepper smirked. "She lives on the edge of the woods, doesn't she? People say she's completely weird, though *obviously* I don't believe that. She's probably perfectly nice, isn't she, Briony?"

Wicked Woods

"Pepper," Tracey began, but the other girl ignored her.

"What? I'm just saying that Briony must be bored. *I* certainly couldn't live like that. Out away from people, forced to live with an… eccentric relative because there's no one else to take me in. I wouldn't want that. I mean, are you really telling me that you don't find Mrs. Edge a bit creepy?"

Briony felt that she did quite well at that point. She did not, for example, lose her temper. She certainly didn't shout at or hit Pepper. After all, she was just a rather stupid little bully, and Briony had seen that there were far worse things in the world. Instead, she stood and headed from the lunch hall without a word, waiting until she reached the corridor before she leant back against the wall, squeezing her eyes shut while taking deep breaths to calm herself.

"Don't let Pepper get to you." Briony opened her eyes to see Claire standing there. "She's just being mean because you're prettier than she is."

Briony hadn't expected the other girl to say anything like that. "Um… thanks."

"Tracey and me are going to the football game later!" and normal service was resumed. "Ross and Bill will be playing! It's going to be great!"

"I'm sure it will be," Briony replied, though she didn't normally watch much football. She would probably be back at home, reading through textbooks. Or maybe persuading her great aunt to teach her one or two ways to deal with vampires.

"So would you like to come?"

"What?" Briony asked, shaken from thoughts of extra staking practice.

"To the football game. Would you like to come? You can sit with me and Tracey, and Pepper will be too busy cheering to be mean. It'll be fun!"

Claire grabbed hold of her while she said it, practically dancing up and down. Saying no, Briony suspected, wasn't optional. At least, it would have been rather like kicking a puppy. Besides, if yesterday she had been complaining that no one liked her, she couldn't very well complain now that someone did.

"Sure," she said, "I'd love to go."

Chapter 5

The football stadium was a little way from the school, not far from the woods. By the time Briony got there, practically everyone else in town had arrived, at least to judge by the number of cars in the parking lot. Aunt Sophie had let Briony borrow the car for the occasion, and Briony was excited enough at the prospect of the big occasion that she hardly thought about the kind of impression she would make showing up in a vehicle that seemed to be mostly held together by the rust.

She found a spot to park in, wedged between an SUV and a pick-up truck, then made her way inside. For what was just a high school football game, there were a lot of people there. Then again, there probably wasn't quite as much to do in a small town like this, and in any case, Briony remembered either Ross or Bill saying that the team had been doing well. People tended to show up when you were winning.

"Briony! Up here!"

Briony hardly had to look to know that it was Claire doing the shouting. She was up in the bleachers, with Tracey beside her. They were both wearing the team's colors, which turned out to be a kind of horrible lilac and green combination, and for a moment Briony felt out of place, given that she had forgotten to even ask what they were. Still, Claire and Tracey scooted over to make room for her.

"That's an… interesting uniform the team have," Briony ventured.

Claire laughed. "It's horrible, isn't it?"

"It was a plan from one of the coaches," Tracey explained. "Apparently, he thought that if the team looked stupid, they'd have to play that much harder to make up for it."

Briony's brow crinkled. "You know what worries me? That actually makes sense."

Tracey shook her head. "Sense? It's *football*. It doesn't have to make sense."

She returned her attention to the field, where Bill, Ross and the others were huddled around, receiving final team instructions. Pepper and the other cheerleaders were off to one side, trying to work the crowd up into a frenzy while the visiting high school's cheerleaders did the same with the other bleachers.

Eventually, the game got under way. It seemed to be a bit of a grudge match, because both teams plowed into each other with even more aggression than Briony might have expected. Even from the start though, it was obvious that Wicked's team had the advantage. Offensively, they ran circles around the defensive line, stealing yards again and again. Defensively, there were so many sacks that Briony actually found herself feeling a little sorry for the opposing quarterback.

Normally, Briony wouldn't have cared much about football. She had been a cheerleader at her old school, but that was about the occasion and the excitement more than the sport itself. Here though, she found herself getting caught up in the atmosphere, as well as by her new friends' infectious enthusiasm for the game. Or at least, for those parts involving Bill and Ross.

Half-time came and went, with Pepper and the rest of her squad putting on the kind of acrobatic cheerleading display that left even Briony impressed. It seemed that the other girl had *some* talents beyond just being unpleasant. Tracey took the time to introduce Briony to a few of the people around her, a bewildering blur of faces and names that she did her best to keep track of, but knew she wouldn't be able to remember an hour later.

Eventually, the home team won, to the fanatical jubilation of the crowd. Even Briony, who hadn't been at the school long enough to really care whether it was winning or not, found herself caught up in the excitement of it all. Claire, who was practically jumping up and down by the end of the match, hugged her.

"We won!"

"We did," Briony agreed.

Claire and Tracey led her down from the bleachers to congratulate Bill and Ross. Claire practically threw herself at Ross, kissing him deeply, while Tracey settled for something a little more restrained with Bill.

"Well done," Briony said, and the boys nodded their thanks.

"There's a victory party after this," Bill said, "are you three coming along?"

Claire and Tracey declared that they were almost instantly. Briony shook her head. "I can't. I have to get back home."

Wicked Woods

Part of her had wanted to give a different answer, but Pepper was looking over, and Briony could see the irritation on her face at the sight of Briony with her friends. She could guess that the other girl would be at the party too, and Briony didn't want to ruin the evening with another argument. Besides, Aunt Sophie would be expecting her back. Briony didn't want to worry her great aunt by staying out without asking her, and if she did ask, Briony already had a pretty good idea of what Aunt Sophie would say.

So while the others were still talking about how they planned to celebrate the victory, Briony set off alone for the car park, seeking out the spot where she had left her great aunt's car. It took a while. One of the minor rules of the universe is that no car, no matter how carefully parked and committed to memory, is ever quite where you thought you left it. As such, Briony had to spend a good ten minutes hunting around the rows of vehicles, probably looking extremely lost in the process.

"Hi, it's Briony, isn't it?"

Briony whirled at the sudden voice. She hadn't heard anyone approach. A young man her own age stood in front of her, wearing Wicked's team colors over jeans with so many rips they barely counted as being there. Briony vaguely remembered him as one of the many people the other girls had introduced her to at some point in the evening.

"Hi," Briony said. "It's… Tom?"

"Tim. No one *ever* seems to get that right."

"I'm sorry," Briony said. "I met a lot of people tonight."

"And now you're looking for your car." Tim took a step closer. "You're in completely the wrong place, you know. It's over there."

He pointed, and just for a second, Briony followed the pointing finger. Then it occurred to her to ask how someone she had met for perhaps five seconds knew which car was hers, and where it was. She turned back towards him, just in time to watch as Tim opened his mouth to reveal fangs.

"Oh, why couldn't you have made this easy for me?" he demanded. "A nice, pretty girl, on her own, who nobody would miss for a while. We could have had such fun. Well, I could, anyway. Now…" he leapt. At least he tried to, but at that point, Briony had the sense to pull the cross around her neck out from under her sweater, brandishing it at the vampire. She had never seen someone try to change direction in midair before, but the boy somehow managed it, edging away with his hand covering his eyes.

"That won't protect you! Some stupid girl hiding behind her cross. What are you going to do? Stand there like that all night?"

"If I have to," Briony said. She started looking around for her car again. She didn't spot it, but that SUV a couple of rows over looked like the one she had parked beside.

"Oh, you're going to try running for it," Tim said. "How sweet." He edged in a circle around Briony, careful not to get too close, but placing himself firmly between her and the car. "What are you going to do now?"

Briony waved the cross at him again. He flinched. "Why don't you just get out of my way?" Briony suggested.

"What, like *this*?"

In an instant, the boy was gone among the cars. Briony knew better than to think that meant he had truly decided to leave her alone. She edged towards her great aunt's car. Once she was inside it, she would be safe. Well, probably.

"I could be anywhere, couldn't I?" The vampire's words seemed to come from all around, bouncing off cars like a hollow echo. "I could be hiding under one of the cars, or waiting behind one. I could be right by your car, or I could be fifty yards away. You won't know until it's too late, Briony."

"Oh, bite me," Briony snapped back, and then realized that it probably wasn't the best thing to say to a vampire. She kept her hand on the cross and scanned the area around her for movement.

"That's the plan, pretty girl. Just come a little closer."

Briony could hear the anticipation in the vampire's voice. He was actually *enjoying* making her squirm like this. Briefly, Briony considered whether she should try making a break for the car. She even dug around in her pocket for the key, clicking on the key fob's electronic opening system to unlock it. She suspected that she wouldn't have time to mess around with keys once she got to the car.

Wicked Woods

"So why me?" Briony demanded, still walking. Maybe if she kept Tim talking, eventually some kind of help would arrive. Though what kind of help might actually be that *helpful*, when it came to vampires, was the real question. At least if he kept talking, Briony supposed she might get some sense of where Tim was hiding.

"Why *not* you?" the vampire countered. "You'll make a nice enough snack. And an easy one too. Alone. Easy to pick off, and it's not like anyone will care if the new girl disappears."

That made Briony's jaw clench. She clutched the cross tighter.

"Oh, angry, are we?" Tim taunted. "Like you could do anything. You can't even spot me sneaking up right behind you."

Briony spun, but she wasn't quick enough. The vampire barreled into her, bearing her to the ground with him atop her, his fangs wide in anticipation of the blood to come. His hand balled in her hair, drawing her head back to expose the line of her throat. Briony couldn't help screaming, but the sound travelled into the night in a way that suggested that there wouldn't be anyone there to hear it, certainly not over all the excitement in the stadium.

She did the only thing she could think of. Putting the base of the cross to the vampire's chest, and hoping that she could remember where the heart was, Briony pressed the secret catch to extend it.

There was a sharp *snick* from the cross, and the vampire pinning Briony gave a kind of gasp before rolling clear of her. Fire seemed to play across him in the dark, blue with a heat that wasn't there as it consumed him. In just seconds, all that was left was a small pile of burnt cinders that no one could ever have recognized as human.

Briony stared at it for a full thirty seconds. Had she just... had she *really*... She scrambled to her feet, sprinting for her great aunt's car. Diving inside, Briony locked the doors behind her, shoved the key into the ignition, and backed out of the parking lot so fast that she nearly ran over a couple of passing football fans. Right then, Briony didn't care.

Chapter 6

Briony had always been very careful when she had been driving. She had listened carefully to the various warnings that went with it, and had tried to make sure she followed them. You shouldn't drink and drive, they said, or drive when you were tired, or angry, or using your cell phone.

To that list, Briony suspected that they should add "don't drive when you have just killed one of your classmates who have turned out to be a vampire." Just because it probably wouldn't come up that often, didn't mean that it wasn't important. At the moment, for example, she was bumping along the roads through the wood with an almost complete disregard for the speed limits, bouncing around in the car every time it hit a pothole and trying to remember the way back to Aunt Sophie's house at the same time.

That wasn't easy. It looked different in the dark, and Briony had to admit to herself that she hadn't been paying a great deal of attention anyway. She was used to places with plenty of signposts, not to mention where there were enough street lights that you could see more than twenty feet in front of yourself at night.

Should she have turned right at that last fork in the road, or was it further on? Briony wasn't sure. She was too busy replaying everything that had happened in the parking lot. The cat and mouse before the vampire had leapt. Being pinned to the ground. Placing the cross over his heart and pressing the hidden catch.

She had just killed one of her classmates. Oh.My.God. But if she hadn't, she would've become his meal. Just the thought of that was enough to make Briony swerve slightly across the road. She tried to concentrate, but it wasn't that easy when the thought of what she had done kept coming back. She had killed him, just like that. Yes, he would probably have killed her if she hadn't, but that didn't really make things much better.

Briony glanced down, and saw that she was doing almost twice the speed she should be. She braked, pulling the car back to a reasonable speed.

The first thing Briony felt was the car's wheels jerking through another pothole. It lost traction on the road as it did so, and Briony panicked, trying to slam on the brakes. She knew she had done the wrong thing when the wheels locked, and the car kept going, off towards the trees.

The crash wasn't a bad one. Had she still been travelling as fast as she'd been going before, for example, it could have been a lot worse. As it was, the car skidded, bumping into a large elm hard enough to bring things to a jolting stop. The world flashed white for a few seconds as the air bag opened then deflated.

Briony sat very still for a second, wide-eyed. She couldn't believe she had crashed…that she had crashed Aunt Sophie's car, and that the air bag went off, but deflated. Briony spent a few more seconds assessing her situation and making sure she wasn't hurt anywhere, and then clambered out of the car to inspect the damage. The front was dented, obviously. As for the rest of it, Briony didn't really know enough about cars to judge whether she should try driving home with it as it was.

A howl cut through the darkness.

Briony scrambled for her cell phone, hoping that she would at least be able to call her great aunt and get help soon. She didn't want to be out in this forest a minute longer than she had to. That feeling intensified when more howls answered the first, and Briony heard the sound of footsteps in the trees beyond the car. The trouble was, a glance down confirmed that there wasn't any reception for her phone so deep among the trees.

It was at that point that things got a lot worse. Briony wasn't sure where the first wolf came from. It had to have come out of the trees while she was still looking down at her phone, because by the time she looked back up, it was already sitting in the road, staring at her. It was a large, brown-coated thing, with intelligent eyes.

Other wolves moved out of the forest to join it, padding out one by one until they sat almost a dozen strong around the car. Around Briony. She fumbled for the cross, taking it out and pressing the hidden catch so that its sharp blade extended. There was still blood on it from where she had stabbed the vampire.

"Who wants to be first?" Briony demanded. She had had *enough* of things wanting to eat her for one day. She let anger fill her up, nearly spilling over the fear as she stood waiting for one of the creatures to make a move. For a moment, at least, the sight of the silver blade seemed to give them pause.

Wicked Woods

A smaller wolf with pale fur leapt first. Briony's old cheerleading training immediately kicked in, and she ducked, bringing the sharp point up like a lance so that it jabbed into the creature's side. The thing's teeth were only inches from her face, and Briony had to use one arm to keep its scrabbling claws from scratching her. She drove the knife in deeper, and it stilled.

Briony pushed the creature away, and it fell limply to the ground. Then, somewhere between one breath and the next, it changed. The fur gave way to skin, the wolf's form to that of a young woman about Briony's age. Briony was sure that she had seen her before. Maybe somewhere at school? Was *anybody* in this place just a normal human?

Briony didn't have time to answer that, because more of the creatures leapt at her. She swung the silver cross left and right, slashing at the advancing creatures, but with so many of them, it was all she could do to keep them from ripping her to shreds. One would feign from one side, and another would lunge in at Briony as soon as she reacted.

Briony felt something grabbing hold of her, and she realized that one of the werewolves had become human again. He gripped her arms with strong hands, pinning them to Briony's sides as she struggled to stab backwards at him. Briony knew that she was in trouble. With a blade in her hands, she could keep him busy trying to prevent her from cutting him, but that was it. It was only a matter of time before one of the other wolves took advantage of it to bite her.

One of them looked like it had the same idea. It was the big, brown furred one from before, which stalked forward, growling as it came. Briony struggled, but her arms were still held firmly. All she could do was hope that it would be quick.

A commotion came from back in the trees, and a young man strode from them, waving a burning branch like it was a sword. It might as well have been, because the werewolves fell back before it, yelping and snarling as their fur singed. The one approaching Briony turned towards him, and found itself knocked away.

This close, Briony could see that the young man was perhaps a little older than she was, with short blond hair and features that almost spilled over from simply handsome into beautiful. He was wearing a dark leather jacket and jeans, along with thick boots that let him kick out at the wolves without getting his leg bitten off.

Wicked Woods

Briony took her cue from him, stamping backwards hard enough that the grip of the werewolf behind her loosened. She stabbed backwards, and felt him stumble away from her. At the same time, the newcomer threw his burning branch at the wolves and dove for the car.

"What are you waiting for?" he demanded. "Get in!"

Briony wrenched open the door on her side, hopping in and closing it after herself. Wolves scrabbled at the windows, snarling and yelping.

"Drive, or we're both dead."

Briony didn't need any more encouragement than that. With a silent hope that the engine would still start after the crash, she turned the key, and almost jumped for joy when the engine started first time. She threw the car into reverse, not caring if she hit any of the wolves. For a moment, it seemed like the battered old Ford might not move, that it might be stuck in the soft ground. Then, like a cork coming free of a bottle, it plunged back onto the road.

Briony spun the wheel sharply, forcing the thing to turn back the way she had come. Switching gear again, she shot off forward as quickly as it would let her, hoping that it would be enough. How fast could wolves run, anyway?

As it turned out, she didn't get to find out. Briony glanced back in the rear-view mirror, and the werewolves were not giving chase. Instead, they sat by the road, just watching as they drove away. Somehow, that seemed more ominous than if they had been sprinting level with her rear bumper.

"So," Briony said, "it's lucky you were passing…"

"Fallon. And you're Briony."

"How did you know that?"

The boy smiled in a way that was simultaneously both deliciously exciting and utterly infuriating, his blue eyes winking. "Would you believe me if I said, 'with my special powers'?"

"*What* special powers?" Briony found herself reaching for her silver cross again.

Fallon laughed. "Sorry, this probably isn't the best moment for that kind of joke, is it? I just heard that there was someone new in town. Now, I haven't seen you before, and you look a lot like the description, so you must be Briony."

Briony sighed. It was nice to have a mundane explanation for once. "Sure. It's just… this has been a weird couple of days."

Wicked Woods

"A werewolf attack is enough to make anyone jumpy. Now, I figure that it's probably best if I show you the way into town, and you can make your way home easily from there. Is that all right?"

Briony nodded, and let Fallon give her directions that ended up with her in the middle of Wicked, not far from George's diner. As they drove, Briony started to notice that her passenger didn't look very well. At least, he was looking paler and shakier by the minute.

"Are you all right?" she asked him. "None of them bit you, did they?"

"No, I... I'm fine. You know your way back from here, right?" When Briony nodded, Fallon opened the passenger side door and started to get out. "Good, then I will get going."

"Are you *sure* you're all right?" Briony asked.

"Completely, but thanks for caring." He slipped out of the car, starting to walk away. It occurred to Briony that there was one thing she hadn't said.

"Thanks for saving... oh." By the time she'd gotten halfway through the sentence, Fallon was already gone.

Chapter 7

Aunt Sophie wasn't too upset about her car, in the end. After all, when you spent your life fighting the forces of darkness, keeping a paint job perfectly intact was never going to be that likely. She was also sympathetic about what had happened in the parking lot, putting an arm around Briony.

"Killing the first one is hard. It gets easier."

Briony wasn't sure if she liked that thought, though to be fair, she liked the thought of being drained by a vampire or torn to shreds by werewolves even less. Yes, she would definitely have to press Aunt Sophie for some lessons in protecting herself from them soon.

She had hardly dared raise the fact that both the vampire and one of the werewolves had been classmates of hers. Briony had been half-afraid that Aunt Sophie would pull her out of the school. Well, that or charge down there with a big vat of holy water. Neither seemed likely to win her friends.

Wicked Woods

She merely told Briony to be careful, and sent her on her way. Briony got to school the next day, and if she found herself a little more cautious around some of the others there, that was only to be expected. In any case, the others were still a little standoffish with her. Claire and Tracey were friendly enough, but generally only when Pepper wasn't watching them closely. The others in her little clique were less willing to risk the wrath of their unofficial queen, and didn't say much to Briony, even if they weren't actively unfriendly.

One side effect of this was that Briony found herself making friends in other places. Partnered up with a short, dark-haired girl with glasses called Maisy for a science lab, Briony quickly found herself liking her, and getting on so well that Maisy invited her to sit with her and her boyfriend Steve when it came to lunch. Steve was good looking in a scruffy kind of way, with a shirt that looked like it had never heard of the concept of being ironed, and sandy-haired that seemed to have a mind of its own. He greeted Maisy with the news that he had finally come up with something that might let him beat her at chess.

"And this is Briony," Maisy said.

"Hi." Steve gave her a thoughtful look. "Hey, weren't you sitting with the popular girls at the football game?"

"I think I only get to hang out with them part-time," Briony replied, and Maisy nodded solemnly.

"They can be really stuck up, sometimes. I don't suppose you like sci-fi, do you?"

She and Steve started to chat about a television show Briony had never heard of. It had too many vampires in it for her taste, given what things were like around Wicked, but she did her best to keep up anyway. The other two kept going without any of the awkward comments that would have shown up around Pepper, and the only slight pause came when they asked her about some math problem that had shown up in a test last week that Briony hadn't been there for. Briony smiled. It seemed that in the absence of the popular crowd, she had been made an honorary geek.

It wasn't nearly as bad as she might have thought, and Briony actually felt a little guilty that at her old school, she probably wouldn't have spent much time talking to girls like Maisy. Now that she was here, Briony resolved never to be that stuck up again. After all, if hanging out with people outside the popular crowd was the kind of thing Pepper Freeman would never do in a million years, it couldn't be all *that* bad.

And then, it got a whole lot better.

Briony didn't see Fallon come into the cafeteria, because she was sitting with her back to the door. In fact, she only noticed him when Maisy looked up and said.

"Hey, who's the cute guy?"

"That would be me, wouldn't it?" Steve countered.

"In your dreams, maybe."

It was good-natured enough, and by that point, Briony wasn't really listening anyway, because she had turned to look. Fallon looked, if anything, even better by daylight than he had last night. Of course, today he didn't have a pack of wolves milling around him, though some of the cheerleaders were doing a pretty good impression of it. Even Pepper got up from her perch at the center of the room and made a beeline for him.

"We were just wondering if you would like to come and sit with us," she said. "It can be hard, making friends when you're new."

"Yes," Fallon agreed, "it can. Thanks for the offer, but I already have a spot." Pepper's eyes widened as he turned and walked over to where Briony sat. Though not as much as Briony's did. "Do you mind if I sit here, Briony?"

"No... sure... I mean..."

"She means sit down," Maisy translated. She smirked in the manner of someone who was filing away for future reference exactly how red Briony had started to go. "I'm Maisy, and this is my boyfriend Steve."

She extended a hand and Fallon took it. "Hello, Maisy. Hello Steve."

Briony was grateful for the pause in which to get her thoughts together. Fallon went to school *here?* Well, of course he did. Where else was there another high school nearby? It was just... well, the other night, he'd seemed a little older than her, not to mention a lot more confident. Briony had a hard time imagining someone like him going to school anywhere. She risked a glance back at Pepper. The cheerleader was looking at Briony in a way that made her glad that looks couldn't kill. Around her, most of the more popular crowd were looking puzzled. Why wouldn't the gorgeous new boy want to sit with them? Only Claire smiled, giving Briony a very discrete thumbs up.

Finally, Briony returned her attention to Fallon. "I didn't realize that you went to school here."

Wicked Woods

"Until today, I didn't. I'm even newer here than you are. Maybe we could take turns showing each other around?"

"You'd only get each other lost," Maisy said.

Fallon shrugged. "Getting lost in a school isn't such a big deal. That forest of yours, on the other hand..."

Briony winced at the casual hint towards what had happened the previous night. "Strange," she said to cover it, "I thought you looked too old to be in high school."

"I'm eighteen," Fallon said, apparently willing to ignore her discomfort. "It just that, if I ever want to get into college, I'm going to have to make up a few classes. Maybe you'll see me in some of them."

Briony caught the hopeful note in it. "Um... maybe."

They chatted some more, and it earned Fallon some points that he talked to Maisy and Steve just as much as to her. He wasn't the kind of guy who would ignore the unpopular kids, then. He even seemed to get a few more of the other two's sci-fi references than Briony did, making a couple of comments about shows that seemed to be sufficiently obscure to impress them.

Eventually though, Maisy made an excuse to leave. Something about having to get to the next class a little early because she wanted to talk to the teacher. At least, Briony assumed it was an excuse. If it wasn't, then the part where she elbowed Steve in the ribs and repeated it loudly and slowly so that he would get the message and go with her was a bit excessive.

"It seems that your friends want to give us some space," Fallon observed. "I think Maisy wants to play match maker."

"Well don't get any ideas," Briony said, though she found herself hoping that he'd had at least a *few*.

"Really?" Fallon raised an eyebrow. "Well, I suppose it would be a bit much to ask for the most beautiful girl in the school to throw herself at me. Tell me, not that I'm complaining, but why aren't you hanging out with all the rest of the pretty crowd?"

He nodded towards where Pepper and the others still sat. She wasn't actively glaring at Briony any more, but she did glance across from time to time. The looks now were more puzzled than anything. Briony could guess what she was thinking. If she had always been able to get attention from any boy she wanted, why was *this* one ignoring her?

"It's not really my scene. Some of them are all right. It's just…"

"Yes, I saw the way the silly rich one looked at you."

"Then you probably saw the way she looked at you too. Tell me, Fallon, why aren't *you* over there with them? I'm sure Pepper would just love to be friends with you."

"She's not really my type."

"Oh, I doubt that," Briony said. "Girls like her are everyone's type."

"In her world, maybe. It's just as well I don't fit in there, then."

That comment raised a warning bell in Briony's head. Around here, not fitting in could mean a lot of things, and what kind of young man could fight off werewolves?

"What were you doing out in the woods last night, Fallon?"

"That's a bit out of nowhere, isn't it?"

"So were you coming to save me," Briony shot back. "Not that I don't appreciate it, but it is a bit of a coincidence, isn't it?"

"Not really," Fallon said. He brushed back a strand of hair. "The woods around here are supposed to be really good for nature walks, so I thought I might try it. I just ended up getting a bit closer to nature than I really wanted with those wolves. What *were* they, anyway?"

"You mean you don't know?" Briony couldn't believe that. Fallon hadn't panicked, the other night, at the sight of werewolves. He hadn't asked questions afterwards. Surely, he wouldn't have been so calm if he hadn't known. So he was lying to her. But why? Briony doubted that he could be some kind of werewolf himself, not after fighting them. But he had seemed sick in the car, and the silver in her cross had been in his proximity.

Fallon sighed, and it was a beautiful sigh, the kind of thing a romantic poet might have managed on realizing that the world contained darker things than flowers and gentle pleasure.

"Briony, look at me."

Briony did it without thinking. It wasn't exactly a hardship. Fallon was amazingly, almost excessively, good-looking with his full lips, wide cheekbones... Briony could have studied the details of his face for hours. His lips, his cheekbones, his eyes...

Wicked Woods

There was something strange about those eyes. They were too pale, so that the irises became almost an extension of the orb. Briony struggled to remember where she had seen eyes like that before. It was something to do with the people who had come to the house, wasn't it? As she stared into Fallon's eyes, struggling to remember, Briony found herself looking deeper into them, and deeper, and…

"Briony," Fallon said, his tone soft.

"Yes?"

"I think it will be better if you forget that you need to know what I am. Better for both of us. Can you do that, Briony?"

"Yes."

"Good. I think what you need right now is a friend, so I want you to trust me, Briony. Wake up now."

Briony shook her head, trying to clear it. "What were you saying?"

"Oh," Fallon said, "nothing important."

Briony doubted that anything he said could be that unimportant, but she decided to leave it. After all, she trusted him.

"Shouldn't we be getting to class?"

Chapter 8

This was the kind of class you didn't get at school, taking place in the backyard of Aunt Sophie's inn, with just Briony, her great aunt, and George from the diner in attendance. George had brought a big bag with him, and he opened it to reveal contents that gleamed silver in the evening sun.

"After what happened the other night," George said, "Sophie has decided that maybe it's time for you to learn to protect yourself."

"Preferably without clanking while she moves, George. Did you *have* to bring *everything*?"

The diner owner shrugged. "There are a lot of weapons for Briony to learn about."

That, it seemed, was true. George spread them out on the back porch like an exhibit from a museum. Monster killing through the ages, possibly. There were stakes and silver-bladed knives, silver wire garrotes and sharpened crosses. There were even swords, short stabbing things that

Wicked Woods

Aunt Sophie said were based on an ancient Celtic design. Their edges gleamed with the familiar silver shine. A couple of elegant, deadly looking crossbows rounded out the collection.

"Crossbows?" Briony said. "Wouldn't guns be better?"

"Shotguns with silver shot can work," George said, "but mostly only on werewolves. A wooden quarrel, on the other hand, is essentially a flying stake."

That made a kind of sense, so Briony went along with it while George and Aunt Sophie discussed the weapons' merits in a matter of fact way.

"Knives and stakes are easy to conceal," Aunt Sophie said, "but hard to explain if you're found with them. I don't fancy my niece going to jail."

George nodded. "You certainly won't be able to carry them around somewhere like your school for instance. There, your cross will have to be enough, though frankly I doubt anyone will attack you on the grounds anyway."

"You can't be too careful," Aunt Sophie shot back. She looked at Briony. "Never assume that you're safe. I don't mean that you should become paranoid, but always be prepared. Danger can be anywhere."

Briony nodded. She had learned that the hard way the other night.

"What are the swords and crossbows for then?" She asked. "You couldn't conceal them, except in maybe a bag, and then you wouldn't be able to get to them in time."

"They are for when we go hunting for the creatures," George explained. "At times like that, you don't have to worry too much about whether people spot the weapons."

"For now though," Aunt Sophie put in, "I would like you to concentrate on the easier to hide options, Briony. We can move onto other things once you have learned enough to defend yourself."

Her great aunt showed Briony some of the best ways to hide weaponry, and how to get to it again in a hurry. Aunt Sophie made a knife appear and disappear with such speed that it was like a conjuring trick, and before long, Briony found that she could at least get to her cross without any trouble. Once she could do that, George suggested that they should move on to some combat techniques.

Wicked Woods

The first stage of that seemed to be taping layers of padding to Briony, and then encasing her head in something close to a crash helmet. Apparently, they weren't planning on holding back. George tossed her a simple stick, taking one for himself and starting to circle around Briony. Over the next five minutes, he threw some simple attacks at her, and Briony found herself beginning to enjoy the process of learning to deal with them.

It was at that point that George sped things up a little.

Briony fought and dodged, swerved and parried. For the moment, at least, it was all she could do to manage that, her own stick engaged in a frantic blur of defense that never quite seemed to be fast enough to stop everything. Only the fact that she currently had more padding strapped to her than the average football player kept Briony from being black and blue.

"Oh come on!" Briony complained as George moved in close, lifted her up, and lowered her not entirely gently to the dirt. "How am I meant to deal with this, Aunt Sophie? George is bigger than me, stronger than me…"

"Let's not forget the unarmed combat training from the army," George added with a smile, "I *was* special forces, after all."

Aunt Sophie shrugged. "Then you'll just have to dodge that much better, won't you? Let's try again."

That wasn't really the answer Briony had been hoping for. In fact, almost nothing about the "training" had been what she had expected. Briony had seen people doing martial arts before, and had half-anticipated standing there practicing movements for hours, or learning clever locks and tricks that would let her fling people around with ease. It didn't seem to be happening so far.

The next round of sparring lasted perhaps ten seconds, before George simply crashed forward, using his greater height and bulk to knock Briony sprawling. She managed to tuck and roll, because there were some things you got good at as a former cheerleader, but even as she got up, Briony found herself knocked down again. This time she decided to stay in the dirt.

"Had enough already?" Aunt Sophie asked lightly.

Briony managed to struggle up to a sitting position. "I can't see any way to win. I'm just getting knocked around here."

Wicked Woods

"I'd prefer to think of it as getting in valuable practice when it comes to falling." Aunt Sophie paused, and shook her head. "You think that this isn't fair then, having to fight someone bigger and stronger?"

Briony knew better than to say that. "I know vampires are going to be stronger, Aunt Sophie," she said instead. "I just don't know what to do about it."

Her great aunt helped Briony to her feet. "So you think that the stronger person always has to win? Well, let's find you a fairer opponent then, shall we? I'm just an old woman, you should be able to overpower me easily enough. Now, want to play?"

Aunt Sophie moved over to the collection of weapons, picking up the swords. She tossed one to Briony, who caught it and experimented with different grips while George strolled back to the porch, leaning against the wall.

"This one is quite a simple game," Aunt Sophie said. "For now, I am the vampire, and all you have to do is kill me. Or touch me above the heart, or throat at least. I'll give actually being impaled or decapitated a miss, if you don't mind."

She stood there. Just stood there. Briony adopted what she hoped was a suitable fighting stance, edging forwards. Aunt Sophie spread her hands, giving Briony a little smile.

"What are you waiting for, dear?"

Something about that smile infuriated Briony. She lunged, aiming straight for the heart. Aunt Sophie barely had to move to slap the sword aside with her own, and her foot took Briony's legs from under her. In a second, she was kneeling by Briony, the blade at her throat.

"If you make it obvious that you're about to fight, then you will lose. The trick is to strike with surprise," Aunt Sophie paused just long enough to trap Briony's arm as she tried to bring the sword up. "*Real* surprise. Nice attempt, Briony. Let's try again."

The next attempt saw Aunt Sophie stabbing out, parrying Briony's blade and thrusting in one motion, placing the point just above her heart.

"Find a way to go on the attack straight away. Vampires do not tire. You cannot wear them down. Every second that the fight goes on is one where they might hurt you more."

On and on the lesson went, with Aunt Sophie finding new ways to defeat Briony each time. Every time, she would offer Briony some piece of advice, whether it was something simple like "pay attention to what your opponent is doing," or something specific like "avoid the whole rush of the attack, not just one movement."

Aunt Sophie didn't seem to tire, though Briony was rapidly becoming exhausted. Where George had been all speed and aggression, Briony's great aunt barely seemed to move. Whether it was with the swords, with knives, or simply with her hands, she always seemed to do the bare minimum needed to deal with whatever Briony was doing while at the same time delivering attacks that would have seriously hurt or killed even most supernatural attackers.

Even when Briony got lucky towards the end of the session, and succeeded in grabbing Aunt Sophie as she tripped her, it didn't make any difference. Her great aunt turned as she fell, scrambled into a better spot, and in seconds had Briony's arm twisted painfully behind her back.

About the only upside to it all was that Aunt Sophie seemed quite pleased with Briony's progress, or at least with her willingness to keep going while being steadily beaten up by elderly relatives. When Aunt Sophie finally called a halt to it all, she patted Briony on the shoulder, told her that it was a good start, and then said that she would go fix some dinner if Briony helped George put the weapons away.

Briony nodded gratefully, then set about the work of collecting up knives, swords, and the occasional silver throwing star. Had they used those? Briony couldn't remember. She was too exhausted from the drubbing her great aunt had given her.

"How did she do all that," Briony asked George.

The diner owner shrugged. "Sophie has been doing this a long time, remember. I suppose, if you spend your life fighting creatures that want to kill you, then you only survive if you get very, *very* good at it."

Briony supposed that made sense, though it was still hard to think of someone who looked like her great aunt being able to throw people around like that. Maybe that was what years of practice did for you.

"Do you think I'll ever be able to fight like that?" Briony asked.

"I don't know," George said. "Given time, and practice, and a lot of thought, you'll certainly get better. But Sophie is something special. You know how people have different talents?"

Wicked Woods

"Like some will be good at football, and others will play music? That kind of thing?"

"Kind of. Mostly, that's just a question of interest. I mean, if you work hard enough at something for long enough, you'll generally get pretty good at it. Some people though, you just know that they are born to do something. Sophie was born to fight. She does it like you or I would walk down the street." George grinned. "Still, if she says she sees something in you, maybe you've inherited the family gift. You've just got to work hard to develop it."

That was reassuring, kind of. Though Briony could think of better areas to be gifted in. And of course, that still left the minor problem in Briony's case that she had already been attacked by both vampires and werewolves. Would she get the *chance* to get as good as Aunt Sophie was, or would she find herself killed long before things got that far?

Briony shuddered at the thought.

Chapter 9

Dinner turned out to be a chicken casserole, which George stayed to share, even though Aunt Sophie complained good-naturedly about him eating enough for three people. Briony tasted it and found that it was one of the best things she had tasted. She said as much.

"Sophie's talents don't just extend to killing things," George said, and Aunt Sophie glared at him.

"Well, *one* of us has to be able to cook properly."

"Oh, so you won't be coming in for any more burgers, then?"

"I might," Aunt Sophie said, "though only to keep an eye on Briony once you give her a job."

"What?" George asked, and Briony found herself echoing it.

"What?"

"Well," her great aunt said, "you *did* drive my car into a tree, dear. And you weren't even being chased by anything at the time. It's really only fair that you should pay for the repairs. Besides, it will do you good to work a little, meet new people, and maybe earn a little extra money."

"And do I get a say in this?" George asked.

Aunt Sophie scooped an extra helping of casserole onto his plate. "Now, George, you know you need the extra help. Jill does her best, bless her, but she can't be everywhere at once. Young Briony here would be a great help to you after school and at weekends, and you know it."

"I suppose you're right," George said.

"I'm always right."

Just like that, it was settled. Briony would start work straight away, going back with George when he left the inn. She would work a few shifts after school, as well as helping out on weekends, when things tended to be busier in town. She noticed that at no point had anyone asked her whether she wanted the job. Still, it wasn't like she particularly minded, the extra money might come in useful, and she *did* feel kind of bad about crashing her great aunt's car.

It would have been even better though if Briony had been able to escape the feeling that her aunt was trying to get rid of her for a few more hours each day. Had she done something wrong aside from the car? Was Aunt Sophie finding it hard to have her around? The last thing Briony wanted was to be a burden.

She actually tried bringing up the subject with George in the car back to the diner the next day after practice, but the ex-soldier just shook his head.

"One thing I've learned over the years with Sophie is that you shouldn't try too hard when it comes to second-guessing her motives. She'll have her reasons."

"I'm just worried that she doesn't want me around," Briony said.

"And what gave you that idea? Sure, Sophie is grieving right now, the same way you are, I'd guess. But that doesn't mean she wants to get rid of you." He pulled up to the diner. "Now, let's get you inside and get you squared away."

"Squared away" entailed finding Briony a black t-shirt to wear at the diner, which proved to be a little too large, taking her on a guided tour of the kitchen, the storerooms, and the various refrigerators, and introducing her to everyone else who worked there.

Wicked Woods

Jill was friendly, in an overworked kind of way, finding time to say hello in between dashing around tables, and assuring Briony that she would get the hang of things there in no time. The kitchen provided two other inhabitants of the diner, in the form of Phil and Percy. Phil was the cook, a wiry, tattooed man in his forties with the same brand of close-cropped hair as George. Percy, his nephew, looked to be about twenty, was skinny and had dirty blond hair that desperately needed a haircut. He served as the dishwasher, busboy, and general gofer around the diner.

Her first shift at the diner was a busy one. So was the one after that, and the one after that too. Over the next few days, things fell into a routine. Briony would go to school, where she would spend her time hanging out with Fallon, Maisy, Steve, and occasionally Claire and Tracey if Pepper's back was turned. After school, Briony would hurry home, get changed, and rush to the diner, where she would work for a couple of hours before heading back to her great aunt. Aunt Sophie would invariably be waiting with dinner, questions about how her day had gone, and a long session of slayer training to get through.

With her days so busy, Briony hardly had time for thoughts of anything else, and maybe that was the point. When being kept so busy, it wasn't easy to dwell on her family, or on the dangers around Wicked, or even on the fact that Pepper still didn't like her very much. The cheerleader had come into the diner once since Briony had started, but Jill had dealt with her order. Briony had been relieved to see that, while someone like Pepper would never condescend to pay someone like Jill any attention, she was at least polite.

That was one of the strange things about Briony's new job. People didn't look at you, except when they wanted something. Even people she knew from school would hardly say anything while Briony was working. It was the closest thing to invisibility Briony had ever come across, though it did at least mean that she could wander around the tables, picking up fragments of conversation and speculating silently on the people who showed up in the diner.

A lot of them seemed to be regulars, which probably said something about the quality of the food. Others were tourists, passing through on their way to better-known spots around Salem. There were many who would come in with slightly worried looks about the décor, but they would generally leave vowing to return on their way back. Phil and George could certainly cook.

From gossiping with Jill and Percy, Briony learned that Phil had been in the army with George, under his command. Briony guessed that he must have liked it, if he were willing to come and work for him afterwards. Jill, she learned, was an only parent, doing her best to look after her young daughter Sarah while trying to earn enough to get by. Percy mostly seemed to be there because he didn't have anything better to do, and Phil, as his uncle, felt that he needed something to keep him out of trouble. Briony couldn't help thinking about what Aunt Sophie had to think about her at that point.

Things went well at the diner. Briony even found that she liked the busy times there, when bigger crowds started to come in and everyone would have to work together to get food out onto the tables. Briony quickly got the hang of all the small jobs that needed doing around the place, and of dealing with customers of all stripes.

Though there were some odd ones.

It was on her first Saturday there that a trio of college students came in, choosing a table near the window.

There were two guys and a girl, all older than Briony, and all a little wild-looking. The girl in particular had frizzy brown hair, big, dark eyes, and the kind of casually clashing clothes that you only got when you threw things on at random. Of the young men, one was wearing a plaid shirt open over a white t-shirt and jeans, and spent most of his time taking his lead from the other, who was a little better dressed, his polo shirt and slacks giving him an almost preppy look.

"Are you ready to order?" Briony asked, summoning up her nicest smile.

"We'll have three burgers, raw," the girl said.

Briony nodded and rushed off to give their order to Phil, though she amended "raw" to "rare", deciding that she couldn't have heard it properly. After all, who would eat raw hamburger? When the meals were ready, Briony took them out. The diner was starting to fill up again. A few regulars were dotted around the place now, and Briony could already guess what they would order. As she put the plates down, she was already calculating how best to get through them.

"Enjoy your meal."

Wicked Woods

There was one new face, in the form of a guy about the age of the three Briony was currently serving. He was very handsome, with dark-hair flowing down to shoulders obviously broadened by plenty of working out, a strong jaw, and vivid hazel eyes that seemed to brood under all that hair. He instantly moved to the top of Briony's to-serve list.

"Hey! This is *cooked!*"

Briony was torn from her thoughts by that, from the girl at the current table.

"I'm sorry?" she said.

"You should be, you stupid little-"

"Carol," one of the guys tried. "It's no big deal."

"No big deal? I asked for mine raw, and this idiot can't even get that right. I should-"

"Here," the young man said, "have mine. It's still nice and pink."

That mollified the girl a little, and Briony flashed a smile in the hopes of defusing things further.

"I'll go and bring you another burger, if you like. I'm sorry, I didn't think that you'd want it quite that raw."

"That's what we *said* wasn't-"

"Carol." This time the college guy held up a hand. "It's an easy mistake to make. Another burger would be great, thanks."

Briony went off to get it, fetching drinks too, on the house to make up for the problem. That got no more than a grunt from the girl there, though the two guys nodded. Job done, Briony went off to serve the others there. The good-looking college guy was definitely next. He smiled as Briony approached.

"Some people don't know how to control their tempers, do they?"

He ordered a salad. Briony went to give Phil the order, and he took it before jerking his head towards one of the kitchen's garbage bags.

"You couldn't take that outside, could you? I haven't had the chance, and Percy doesn't seem to be around today. I tell you, I worry about that boy sometimes."

Briony wanted to point out that she wasn't exactly taking things easy herself, but that wasn't the kind of thing you said to people you worked with, and anyways, she had just started. So she took out the trash, hauling it around to the dumpsters behind the diner. It at least meant that she had a minute away from the rush.

"Now look what we have here."

Briony turned, and found herself facing the girl who had complained about her burger. Carol, was it? She must have followed her outside. But why would she?

"Stupid little girl. Can't even get simple things right."

"Look," Briony said, raising her hands, "I'm really sorry about that."

"You will be," Carol growled, and it *was* a growl. Carol's eyes narrowed, and she fell to the ground. In a second, she had changed, leaving a wolf where she had been standing. A wolf with shimmering fur that then leapt straight at Briony.

Briony scrambled for her cross, moving automatically after all the drills with her great aunt. The trouble was, a few days didn't make her any kind of expert, and the wolf was already mid-leap. It slammed into Briony, knocking her backward so that she fell with it on top of her, its slavering jaws just inches away. Briony abandoned the attempt to get to a weapon, concentrating instead on just keeping those teeth away from her. And, as they moved steadily closer, Briony knew it wasn't going to be easy.

Chapter 10

And just like that, it was easy. Carol was yanked off Briony in a rush. The sudden release of the wolf's weight came as a shock. The handsome college guy with the dark hair and hazel eyes had just picked up the wolf by the scruff of the neck, flinging it at the far wall of the alley, where it hit with a yelp before changing back into the girl, Carol. She staggered, holding onto the wall for support, but by that time, Briony had her silver cross in her hand, the point extended. Carol took one look at it and ran.

Briony wasn't in the mood to run after her. Instead, she put her weapon away and let the cute guy help her to her feet.

"Ok, so you're not shocked by the sight of a werewolf," Briony said.

"Nor are you. I see from the cross that you're a hunter too."

"Trainee."

He was obviously another member of the Preservation Society. "You must work out a lot to be able to fling a wolf around like that."

"A bit."

That wasn't much of an answer, but Briony let it go. Besides, there was nothing wrong with modesty, even if the simple breadth of the young man's shoulders made it clear that he didn't have much to be modest about in that regard.

"More than a bit. I'm Briony." She held out her hand, and her rescuer took it.

"I'm Kevin. Are you ok?"

"I'll be fine," Briony assured him, though one thought did strike her. Had the werewolf drawn blood? Was there a chance that she was infected? She looked down hurriedly, struggling to breathe. What if she became one of them? What could she do? Aunt Sophie would be *furious.* Actually, Aunt Sophie would probably come after her with a silver-loaded shotgun. Briony ran her hands over herself like someone swarming with fire ants.

"Briony." Kevin's hands caught her wrists, forcing her to stillness. "Calm down. I don't see any cuts. You're perfectly safe."

Wicked Woods

Briony let out a sigh that was deeper than she had intended. "Sorry, I must look really stupid."

"There's nothing stupid about being scared. Particularly not if you think you might become a werewolf. There aren't many things worse than thinking you might end up one."

"You sound like you know," Briony said. "You've hunted a lot of them?"

Kevin paused, and then shook his head. "Not exactly, but I know some of them. Carol there was probably ok before she was infected. You end up having to fight your temper all the time. And your hunger. It isn't easy."

That sounded odd, and it took Briony a moment to realize that she hadn't expected to hear sympathy there. After all, hunters hunted monsters. They didn't empathize with them. Briony could just imagine how badly Aunt Sophie might react if she heard someone being so sympathetic towards the creatures. She would probably hit the roof.

And yet... didn't it make sense to have some sympathy for them? Briony guessed that many werewolves and vampires didn't have the choice about becoming what they were. How would Briony like it if she were to suddenly start turning furry and having to deal with the urge to bite people? Not that Aunt Sophie would ever give her the chance.

"Are you sure you're ok?" Kevin asked. "Only you faded out there for a moment."

"Sorry, just thinking," Briony said.

"Somehow, I doubt it." Kevin grinned showing his perfectly white teeth. He had to know how good-looking he was, to get away with smiling like that. "I've got to be going. I have things I should be doing."

"Chasing monsters, throwing wolves about and rescuing damsels in distress?"

"Laundry, mostly."

Well, presumably even heroic rescuers had to do that kind of thing sometimes. Briony nodded towards the diner.

"Are you sure you won't come back inside? Whatever you want is on me. It's the least I can do after that."

Kevin shook his head, glancing down at his watch. It was a rugged thing that looked like it had been through the wars. "No, I really do have to get going. Thanks for the offer though. I hope you're all right."

Wicked Woods

With that, he left, going back down the alley and disappearing from sight. Briony thought about going after him. But what would that achieve? Besides, she had to get back to-

"Briony! Where are you? You're supposed to be taking out the trash, not stopping to read *War and Peace*!"

Briony sighed, and headed back into the diner. Phil was waiting for her.

"Where have you been? There are customers waiting."

"Sorry. Small werewolf emergency."

There probably weren't many people Briony could say that to in the expectation of any sympathy. Phil the cook was one of them, thankfully.

"Oh. Why didn't you call out? I would have come and helped."

"There wasn't time. Besides, I had help, and it's fine now."

"You weren't bitten, were you?"

Briony shook her head, and tried not to pay attention to the way Phil's hand was creeping towards a rack of knives. "I'm fine. Just a bit shaken up. Hardly even that."

The cook nodded. "That's good. Still, it's best to be careful. Now, can you get back out there? We have three tables waiting to be served."

That, Briony would ponder afterwards, was the thing about vampires and werewolves and the rest of it. They didn't stop normal life. At least, they didn't stop what passed for normal life in the diner. You could be as badly shaken up as you wanted about nearly having been bitten, but table four still needed more fries, and the old guy at table six still wanted to hear all the specials before settling on the burger that he always had.

In a way, it was comforting. No matter how odd things got, there would always be one little corner of the world where the biggest problem was whether Percy had remembered to bus the last table properly, and whether the customers' orders were coming out correctly.

Thinking of that, Briony looked over to the table where Carol and her two companions had sat. The young men were gone, suggesting that perhaps the female werewolf had doubled back as they had left. Presumably, they had been werewolves too. After all, who else ate raw hamburgers?

Wicked Woods

If they were, then they had been a lot nicer than their friend. Which begged the question once more of whether all these creatures were as evil as they seemed. If they didn't have at least some control, then wouldn't it be impossible for them to hide? Wouldn't they be rampaging out in the open, rather than hiding in the shadows? Despite her fears about Aunt Sophie's reaction, Briony resolved to ask her about it once she got back to the inn.

It didn't go quite as badly as Briony had thought. Aunt Sophie didn't actually hit the roof, for example, though she did give Briony a careful look and sat her down at the kitchen table.

"You're asking if werewolves and vampires can ever be good?"

"I suppose so," Briony said. She related what had happened that day.

"One of them attacked you, Briony."

"And two of them didn't. They were actually kind of nice. At least, one of them tried to calm the female one down."

"But he didn't do anything to stop her when she came after you," Aunt Sophie pointed out. "He could just have been trying to make sure that nothing happened in a public place. Remember, they aren't stupid."

Briony nodded, even so, she couldn't help wondering. "It's just that they seemed so normal, and if anyone can get infected, then that must mean at least some good people do."

"That's true," Aunt Sophie said. She moved over to the kitchen counter, turning on the kitchen's kettle. "And maybe you're right. I have thought about this a lot over the years. Maybe they are just nice, ordinary people in an awkward situation. But one thing they will never be is normal."

"No?"

"Think about it, Briony. They become what they are, and suddenly they have a whole world of new hungers and instincts to deal with. It's too much for most of them. For almost all of them. That is why we hunt them. They might not want to hurt anyone now, but can we say that a week from now, or a year, they won't be ripping someone's throat out?"

It seemed a harsh way to put it, but Briony thought back to the vampires and werewolves that had attacked her since her arrival in town. Whatever they had been when they had been human, when they had attacked, they had been ruled by far darker instincts.

Aunt Sophie took her hand. "It can be hard, at first. You find yourself thinking of them, and what it must be like to be hunted down. Be strong though. Remember what it must be like for their victims. For the people who just… disappear."

Aunt Sophie didn't actually say "for your parents" but Briony knew that was what she meant. She was right, of course. How could you trust someone when you knew what they might do at any moment? You couldn't. Even so, there was a part of Briony that rebelled at the idea of just hunting people down and killing them. How did that make them any better than the monsters?

"It's good to see that your lessons are paying off, anyway," Aunt Sophie said. "Fighting that werewolf off without a scratch. Well done."

"Um…," muttered Briony, shifting uncomfortably. "Actually, I didn't do it alone. I was in a lot of trouble until another hunter showed up."

"What other hunter?"

"His name's Kevin. You must know him. He's kind of tall, and broad-shouldered. Dark-haired. He picked up that wolf like it was nothing. He must spend a lot of time training."

Briony knew the moment Aunt Sophie looked puzzled that something had to be wrong.

"Kevin, you say?"

"That's the name he gave me. Why, is there something wrong? Is he, like, someone I shouldn't be hanging around?"

"It's not that," Aunt Sophie said. "It's just that, as far as I know, the Wicked Woods Preservation Society doesn't have anyone in it named Kevin."

Chapter 11

There wasn't much point, in the end, in speculating on who Kevin might be. He had shown up, he had saved Briony, and there was no reason to suspect that she would ever see him again. Admittedly, there was a part of her that felt a little disappointed by that last thought, but Briony did her best to quash it. She even went along with it when her great aunt suggested that what she probably needed was an early night, heading to sleep a good couple of hours before she normally would have.

For some reason, perhaps the part where Briony had laid awake thinking about werewolves and vampires, angry girls in diners and strange young men who came along just when she needed them, the early night didn't exactly refresh her. She went to school feeling almost as tired as she had on her first day there.

Maybe that was why Briony missed the posters at first, though given how brightly colored they were, and the way they were plastered across every available surface, it seemed hard to believe that she could have. Briony stopped, reading. It was an announcement for the school's homecoming dance, a week away, written in bright tones that made it hard to look at.

"I don't know why you're looking at that." Briony hadn't heard Pepper approach. "It's not like anyone would be stupid enough to want to go with you. Or maybe you're going to go with those freaks you call friends? Make a threesome of it? I'm sure you would make a perfect third wheel."

Briony sighed. She didn't need this. "Whereas you will, no doubt, be the center of attention."

"Of course." Pepper stepped closer. Without her entourage around her, she seemed smaller, but not much nicer. "I know you're jealous. A jealous little hopeless pathetic new girl with no family but a crazy aunt."

A flash of anger spiked through Briony then, and her fists clenched. After everything Aunt Sophie had taught her, it would be so easy to teach this stupid girl a lesson in manners. Unfortunately, Pepper spotted what was on the horizon.

"You're actually thinking about hitting me, aren't you? Go ahead. I would love to see you suspended. Maybe even arrested. Maybe you would make some friends who were more your type down in the jail, rather than hanging around here, trying to pick up *my* friends."

The important thing, Briony knew, was to stay calm. It was a lot easier now that Pepper had given her a clue what this was really about.

"You don't like the thought that people might like someone other than you, do you? What is it? Afraid that given a choice, the people you've been pushing around will go elsewhere?"

Pepper's eyes flashed, and she brought one hand around in what was probably meant to be a slap. Briony caught her wrist easily, not striking out, not twisting it. Just holding it while looking at Pepper as levelly as she could.

"Go away, Pepper. Just go away."

The other girl twisted against Briony's grip for a moment, but she wasn't strong enough to break it. Typical. The one person Briony wished was a real monster, wasn't. Briony stared angrily into Pepper's eyes. Just months ago before her family's disappearance when Briony's high school life seemed perfect, she was like Pepper, the Queen Bee of her school. All that can change in a matter of minutes. Though Briony was never mean to others just for the sake of being mean, she understood Pepper…the insecurity that comes from not being the prettiest, the best, the center of attention. Briony left it just a second longer before letting go.

"I'll get you for this," Pepper promised, and Briony shook her head.

"No, you won't. Or do you think it would go down well with the principal, learning that you've been bullying me?"

"No one would believe you."

Pepper hurried off anyway, and Briony let out a breath she didn't know she had been holding. That was the thing about people like Pepper. They were only strong so long as you let them be. They certainly didn't like the thought that their actions might have consequences. Briony doubted that she would try anything again soon. If she did, Briony would welcome the chance to show Pepper not to mess with a slayer.

Not that it made her feel much better. Briony trudged along the halls to her locker, opening it with a leaden clang. Pepper was right. She would be on her own this homecoming. Once, Briony had looked forward to that kind of dance in the knowledge that it would be the most important social night of her year. Now… how many guys would risk the wrath of Pepper by asking her out? How many guys even knew her enough to want to?

"Hello, Briony." Fallon stepped up next to her with a warm smile.

"Is this the day for people sneaking up on me or something?"

"Who else has done it?"

"Oh, just Pepper. She was… being her usual self, I suppose."

Briony felt tears sting her eyes, and she started to turn away from Fallon. His hand brushed her cheek, turning Briony back to face him.

"Hey, what is it?"

"Nothing," Briony tried.

"This," Fallon countered, brushing a tear away with his thumb, "is *not* nothing." He took Briony by the hand, leading her to a seat and crouching beside her. "Now, are you going to tell me what's wrong? I can't imagine it is just Pepper. There's no way someone as stupid as that would get to you on her own."

Briony wasn't sure. Pepper was more than nasty enough. But Fallon was right about one thing. There was more than just that swirling around in her head. "It's this, Fallon. All of this. This place. This town. It's so crazy, and so dangerous."

"It's all of that," Fallon agreed.

"And I wouldn't mind that on its own," Briony added, "if everything else could make some kind of *sense*. But it doesn't. Things just keep piling up. There's moving here, and Pepper, and things attacking me for no reason, and my family…"

Briony tailed off as more tears came. Fallon took her hand.

"I met them, you know," he said.

"You did?"

"I was staying up at the Edge Inn for a few days. I didn't hear that they had disappeared until afterwards, but it was terrible news. They seemed like nice people. They kept an eye on my brother and me. I'm sorry."

Briony didn't know what to say to that. She didn't think that she could talk about her family without more tears making an appearance, and she didn't want to do that in front of Fallon, let alone the rest of the school. She concentrated instead on the other thing there.

"You have a brother?"

Wicked Woods

Fallon was silent for a moment. "I hope so."

"What does that mean?" Briony asked.

"He went missing around the same time as your parents. I haven't been able to find him since."

"That's..." Briony didn't have the words.

Fallon smiled wanly. "It is, isn't it?"

"And you've been looking for him?" Briony asked. "That's why you are really in town? Not something about making up classes?"

Fallon shrugged. "With so many dangerous creatures around, I needed an excuse that wouldn't attract attention. And I *do* need the extra credit. This way, I get to stick around, no one bothers me, and I can keep searching. Though I'm beginning to think-"

Briony put a finger to his lips to silence him. "Don't say it. There is always hope."

Fallon shook his head. "If there is one thing I have learned since coming here, Briony, it is that there is almost never hope. Not for me, anyway."

Briony sighed. What a pair they made, joined together in gloominess. And no wonder Fallon didn't want much to do with the popular crowd. That kind of bright, pointless chatter was exactly the kind of thing that would grate on Briony in her current state, and she couldn't imagine that things could be much better for Fallon. Losing a brother like that. Knowing that he was probably dead.

"There is one upside," Fallon said.

"What's that?"

"At least I know how you feel, Briony. You aren't alone. Though somehow I suspect that you could never truly be alone."

"What does that mean?" Briony found herself becoming defensive. Did Fallon mean that she was one of those shallow, attention-seeking types like Pepper?

"I just mean that you have already attracted friends to you, Briony. Those girls who come over from Pepper's little group to talk to you. Maisy, Steve... me. I know you're used to more than that, to adulation and respect, but is that such a good thing? Me, I'd rather have real friends any day."

That was probably true, Briony thought. Of course, she also suspected that Fallon could have his pick of any friends he wanted. She had already seen how most of the other girls in the school looked at him. Even most of the guys got along with him. Besides, as great as Briony's new friends were, that still left one or two problems.

Wicked Woods

"What is it?" Fallon asked, and Briony guessed that something must have shown on her face.

"I'm just thinking that friends are great, but Maisy is hardly going to lend me Steve for the homecoming dance, and Claire, Tracey, Ross and Bill will probably be going together. Pepper was right about that. I can either go on my own or end up spoiling the party for someone else."

Fallon stood, drawing Briony to her feet as he did it. "That one is easily solved." He smiled warmly, his blue eyes staring into hers. "Would you like to go to the dance with me, Briony?"

"Oh no... Fallon, I couldn't ask you to-"

"You're not. I'm asking you. That's how these things work, isn't it?"

Briony knew that she couldn't just stand there and let him do that. "Fallon, this is incredibly kind of you, but I know there must be plenty of people who want to go with you. I'm not going to have you asking me just because it is what you think you should do. I'm not going to be some kind of pity date because of everything that has happened to me recently."

"Briony?"

"Yes?"

"Would you mind coming to your senses for a moment, please?"

"What? I don't understand."

Fallon looked at her oddly, his head to one side. "You really don't, do you? What I mean is that I'm not asking you to the dance because of your family, or because you don't have anyone to go with, or even because it might be fun to see the look on Pepper Freeman's face when we show up together."

"You aren't?" It probably said a lot about the state Briony was in at the moment that she was even asking. Once, she might have taken it for granted that the gorgeous guy would want to go out with her. Not at the moment.

"No. I'm asking you to the dance because I want to, because you are the most beautiful girl in this school, because you're one of the only ones I can talk to, that I can relate to…considering our families, and because I find you irresistible. So how about it? Will you go to the dance with me?"

Briony didn't have to think about it for long. Fallon was so kind, and perfect, and thoughtful. It also helped that he was the most handsome boy in school, probably all of Wicked. The only guy who had come close to rivaling

Wicked Woods

Fallon's looks, but in a darkly different way, had been Kevin, the college guy from the diner. When Briony thought of Kevin with his dark masculine good looks, she actually blushed. What was the chance that he would ask her out, let alone be back in town? He wasn't standing in front of Briony, asking her out now, while Fallon, with his gorgeous blonde Viking king looks, polite manners, and sweet smile was standing inches away from her, looking intently into her eyes, waiting for her answer.

"I would love to."

Fallon's face moved closer then and his lips was soft against hers. Briony wrapped her arms around his neck, while his arms found its way around her waist pulling her close. They stood like that kissing for how long, she didn't know, but she felt safe within his arms as safe and secure as she hadn't felt in a long time. When they finally pulled back, both of them were breathless. Fallon reached out a finger to trace her face, and look into her eyes. "You don't know how much I wanted to kiss you," he said. "Ever since I've seen you months ago…"

Chapter 12

The days to homecoming passed, for Briony, in a haze of excitement and activity. She briefly saw Fallon every day at school and each time they met, they have had stolen kisses here and there. Fallon was one of the best kissers Briony have had, not that she had many, but he always left her feeling breathless and wanting more after they kissed. Briony was definitely falling for Fallon, whose presence near her was always comforting and secure, yet there was something there, too. Since the day of their first kiss, Briony had wondered what he meant by wanting to kiss her months ago? Until that day, she had only known Fallon for a few weeks, not months. But Briony never got around to ask him what he meant, as her days got busier and busier, and she quickly forgot about it. There was her schoolwork, her work at the diner, and the continued presence of her lessons with her aunt, but new things vied for her attention too.

Wicked Woods

There was the task of finding the right dress, for one thing. Briony certainly didn't have anything to wear in her closet. Aunt Sophie was unexpectedly generous on that score, saying that she would pay for one and sending Briony off into town to find something that would work. When Briony suggested that Aunt Sophie might like to help her look, the older woman lit up, and they spent most of a day trailing around looking for something perfect.

What they actually found was Maisy, trying on dresses that didn't really suit her in one of the local stores, and frowning while she did it.

"Why does nothing look right?" she demanded, as Briony passed. "It's me, isn't it? I'm too short and nerdy to ever look good."

Briony put an arm around her. "You look fine. It's just a question of finding something that suits you. Come on. I'll help."

They had a great time then, trying on different things, and to Briony's surprise, Aunt Sophie seemed fine with Maisy around. If anything, she seemed happy that Briony was getting along with someone, and she actually chipped in with some fashion advice for Maisy too, though she spent most of her time skimming through the racks of clothes looking for something for Briony.

The results were impressive. Maisy twirled in a pretty green dress that made her look almost delicate, smiling broadly. It was the happiest Briony had seen her. As for the dress Briony's great aunt passed her...

It was dark, and sleek, and fell almost to floor length in a swirl of pleats and folds. Above them, it gathered tightly with silver embroidery across the bodice and shoulders, leaving Briony's arms bare. When she tried it on, her hair spilled across it, its lightness a highlight against the black of the fabric.

"How do I look?" Briony asked. Maisy actually gasped. Even Aunt Sophie nodded.

"Beautiful, dear. Come and see in the mirror. You too, Maisy."

Standing beside one another it was like a study in contrasts. Maisy looked like a delightful fairy in the brightness of her dress. Beside her, Briony looked like a blonde princess as elegant and poised as she had ever dreamed of looking. She tried to imagine herself dancing with Fallon in this dress. Yes, she thought, they would certainly draw a few stares.

That thought made her hesitate.

"Um… you don't think that it's a bit too much, do you?"

"I'd rather have that than there being too little of it," Aunt Sophie said primly, but then smiled. "You're thinking of how some of the other girls will react?"

Briony bit her lip. "One other girl, mostly."

Maisy grabbed her arm. "Oh, you have to wear it! It's perfect for you. And Pepper will be far too busy being homecoming queen to bother."

"She's homecoming queen?" Briony asked.

"She's *always* homecoming queen. You know this is the right dress, Briony."

"Your friend is right, dear," Aunt Sophie added. "Besides, I have just the shoes to go with it. They should fit you perfectly."

That seemed to be that. Briony would go to the ball. She wondered for a moment if Cinderella's godmother had been quite so brisk and determined. She also found herself wondering what kind of shoes Aunt Sophie could possibly own that would go with *this* dress.

They turned out to be black. Very, very black. And also tall. That had a lot to do with the heels, which were some of the highest Briony had seen, and which tapered to sharp looking points.

"Wooden heels, of course," Aunt Sophie said. "Just in case there's a repeat of what happened at the football game. One kick with these, and there's no more vampire."

"One night dancing in them, and there's probably no more ankles."

"You'll be fine," Aunt Sophie promised. "Now, shouldn't you be getting off to the diner?"

That was the thing about the build up to homecoming. Real life didn't stop. It just acquired new reasons to be busy. Because Claire and Tracey wouldn't stop pestering her until she agreed, Briony found herself signing up to help out with homecoming when it came to getting things ready. Because Pepper was involved in the organizing committee, that mostly meant the boring jobs, like blowing up several hundred balloons. Even so, Briony noticed that the other girl was starting to keep her distance.

The wait for homecoming seemed to last forever. There were so many jobs to be done, so many other things that demanded Briony's attention. There was a test in Math, which Briony did well...thanks to all the time spent hanging around with Maisy, who had the best grades in class. There was stocktaking down at the diner, which involved a couple of hours spent with a clipboard and a flashlight in one of the storerooms, trying to remember not to hit Percy when he decided to try and startle Briony by jumping out on her.

When the night finally came, Briony felt like she had been waiting for it for years. And here it was, rushing up on her almost too fast. Fallon would be at the house in less than an hour, and she still needed to get ready. That took time. Briony wanted to look perfect, because this was bound to be a special night. Eventually though, she was nearly there, needing only to strap on Aunt Sophie's shoes when the sounds of an argument downstairs floated up to her.

Were they under attack? Was something else wrong? Briony thought she could hear Fallon's voice. Picking up the shoes, she ran down, heading for the hallway.

Aunt Sophie was there, holding her silver cross at arms length. Fallon was there too, wearing a tuxedo that would probably have fitted him perfectly had he not been crouched in a corner, one hand over his eyes.

"Vile creature! Coming near my niece! It's time for you to die!"

Even as Briony watched, her great aunt pressed the catch on her cross that made its sharpened point extend. Briony rushed forward without thinking, raising her shoes in a parry that caught the descending blade.

"Aunt Sophie? What are you doing?"

"Out of the way before he kills us both, you foolish girl."

"Kill us? Why would Fallon kill us?"

"Because your date is a *vampire*, of course!"

Briony wanted to tell her great aunt that she was being stupid, and that of course Fallon wasn't a vampire. Two things stopped her. One was the thought that Aunt Sophie probably wouldn't react that well to being called stupid the next time they sparred together. The other, more important consideration was that Fallon was still cowering back from the cross. It *might* have been because no one, vampire or otherwise, reacts well to the thought of being stabbed through the heart, but somehow, Briony found herself doubting it.

"You're a vampire?"

"Briony, I-"

Wicked Woods

"I want the truth, Fallon, and I want it now." Briony could hear the coldness of her own voice.

Fallon stood still, suddenly looking sad. After a pause, he looked up, meeting Briony's clear direct eyes. "Yes. I'm a vampire." Fallon stood straight, handsome as ever in his black tuxedo with a wry smile that had rather more in the way of fangs than Briony remembered. "I'm sorry."

"You will be!" Aunt Sophie promised, hefting the silver blade again. Despite the leaden feeling in her stomach, Briony shoved her great aunt back.

"Stop this! Just stop this!"

"Briony-"

"And you shut up too, Fallon! I need to think!"

How long she stood there, her hands balled into fists, Briony didn't know. Thoughts swirled around in her. How could Fallon not have told her? But how could he, once he knew who she was? He had saved her, hadn't he? Or was that all part of some bigger plot? Was Aunt Sophie right? *Should* they kill him?

"This explains why you were hanging around with me rather than the popular girls, at least," Briony said, and there was more bitterness there than she intended.

Fallon looked hurt, or was that just another act? "Briony, it's not like that."

"Then what *is* it like?"

"You aren't seriously going to listen to him, are you?" Aunt Sophie demanded.

"Yes. I... can't you see that I *want* to believe him?"

"I wanted to believe a vampire once. It didn't end well." Aunt Sophie paused, and then sighed. "Oh, very well. Why have you been hanging around my niece, vampire?"

Fallon looked from Aunt Sophie to Briony and back. Briony could almost see him trying to work out what might work.

"Don't lie," Briony said. "Please, whatever else you do, don't lie now."

Fallon nodded. "Then the answer to that, at least at first, is because her father asked me to."

Aunt Sophie looked affronted. "Joseph asked you to stalk his daughter? She wasn't even here with the rest of her family. Or are you saying that he's still..." she didn't finish it.

"I don't know, Mrs. Edge. The last I saw of them was in the woods, the night they... the night my brother..."

Wicked Woods

"It's all right, Fallon," Briony said.

He shook his head. "It's not. It's *really* not. That was the night *this* happened to me too. Before that, Joseph...Briony's father and I were separated from the others. He told me that if he... didn't make it, I needed to make sure his family were all right."

"He *meant* his wife and son," Aunt Sophie said. "And I see you failed there."

Fallon looked down. "Yes, I did. I couldn't even save myself. That night was all confusion and chaos. I lost track of Joseph, Mary, Jake, and Pete. I lost track of my own brother. They...the vampires turned me before I knew what was happening. I'm sorry to break the news to you, but I still don't know what happened to everyone. The only thing I knew was that I made a promise to Joseph. And then, I heard that his daughter, Briony, had come to live with you, and I... I knew what I had to do."

"And where did you hear that?" Aunt Sophie asked.

"You know where, Mrs. Edge. Aren't some things best left alone?"

Briony saw her great aunt glance to her. "Maybe you're right."

"And that's all it was?" Briony asked. "You wanted to look after me? Fallon, I told you that I didn't want a pity date. I *certainly* don't want a bodyguard."

Fallon shook his head. "It stopped being that the moment I saw you, Briony…looking so sad and lost, but still proud and beautiful… But I know you have no reason to believe me. Actually, I know you have good reason to just stake me with those… shoes…"

"That was the plan," Briony said, and she couldn't help a small smile. It came along with an answer. "No. That *is* the plan. Come on, Fallon. You're taking me to the homecoming dance."

"Briony!" Aunt Sophie looked incandescent. "I *cannot* allow you to go to the dance with a *vampire!* He might do anything."

"He might have done anything at any point in the last few days too," Briony pointed out. "But he hasn't. I'm not asking you to trust Fallon, Aunt Sophie. I'm asking you to trust me. Trust that I can make this decision."

Aunt Sophie looked between them. "I could just stake him now."

"You'd have to go through me to do it," Briony said. Her great aunt's eyes narrowed.

- 137 -

Wicked Woods

"No, Briony," Fallon said. His grip on her shoulders was gentle, but inexorable as it moved her to one side. "I won't let you get hurt in this."

Briony wanted to tell him that he didn't *let* her do anything, but she had the sense to pause. Aunt Sophie was looking thoughtful, a sudden change in her whole stance and expression.

"Interesting. Fallon... Fallon... are you the boy who stayed here with his brother?"

"I am, ma'am."

Aunt Sophie nodded. "As I recall, you were a polite enough boy. And you have been kind to my niece this last little while. Very well. You may go to the dance with her. Have Briony back before midnight though, or I *will* kill you."

Chapter 13

The drive to the dance was a quiet one. Briony had been so quick to tell her aunt that she would be going, but now, she couldn't help feeling at least a little nervous. She felt guilty for that. Fallon was *Fallon*. He had spent most of the past couple of weeks around her, and it wasn't like he'd ripped her throat out even once.

They stopped just short of the school hall, and Briony saw Fallon patting his pockets, as though he were looking for something. He finally found it, in the shape of two boxes. The first turned out to be a corsage, pale white against the darkness of Briony's dress once she put it on. It went with it so well that Briony had to wonder if he'd known what she would be wearing.

"Maisy told me," Fallon explained without being asked. "I think she wanted this to be perfect. I don't know if there's much chance of that now though."

Wicked Woods

"We can try," Briony said, reaching out for his hand. "After all, it's not like you're about to lunge over and bite me, is it?"

Fallon was silent just a little too long.

"Fallon?"

"The hunger is there, Briony. It's always there. So soon after being transformed, I need a lot of blood. I have been feeding on animals, things I could catch, lesser things. But it is barely enough, and you look so… tempting tonight."

Briony edged back in her seat, just a little. She needed something to distract Fallon, and she needed it quickly.

"What's in the other box?"

"What? Oh, right. I had forgotten." Fallon opened the second box, which was much smaller than the first. Gold gleamed inside it. "You'll have to take it out. I can't."

It was a crucifix. A small, golden crucifix. It hung from a chain of fine, golden links as Briony drew it out of the box. Fallon had his eyes firmly shut.

"Why would *you* buy me this?" Briony wondered aloud. "It doesn't make sense."

"I wanted you to be safe. Even from me. Here, if I keep my eyes closed, I can probably help you to put it on."

Briony thought about pointing out that she already had the silver slayer cross George had given her, although it didn't go well with her dress. She wasn't wearing it though, and had it neatly tucked into her silver evening bag.

Fallon slipped the chain around her neck, fastening the clasp by feel. The movement brought him so close that Briony could smell the clean scent of the soap he used. Funny, she had almost been expecting an undertone of blood. The necklace, once it was in place, hung low enough to be partially hidden by Briony's dress. Fallon pulled back and opened his eyes.

"Well," Briony joked, "at least I know you won't be looking anywhere you shouldn't."

"There is that," Fallon said. "We should go in now. I think everyone else should get at least a brief chance to see how wonderful you look tonight."

"You don't exactly clean up badly yourself."

Apparently, other people thought the same, because they attracted more than their fair share of stares as they walked into the dance together. The festivities were already in full swing, with the dance floor crowded with couples.

Wicked Woods

Maisy was off in one corner with Steve, who didn't seem to be having much success when it came to dancing. A quick glance around the rest of the floor revealed Claire, in a short dress that had probably cost a lot more than it appeared to, and Tracey, in the kind of overblown, glittery thing that only she could ever have gotten away with wearing. Ross and Bill, dancing with them, didn't seem to mind.

Pepper was in the middle of a group of admirers, already wearing the homecoming queen's crown at the top of an ensemble that looked like it tried just a little bit too hard. Briony didn't feel any disappointment at that. Everybody had who it would be, and in any case, maybe it would be a good thing. If Pepper had a clear sign that she was still popular, maybe she wouldn't feel quite so threatened by Briony's presence. Her homecoming king was one of the jocks from the football team. Briony didn't know his name.

"Would you like to dance?" Fallon asked.

"Is this the part where you turn out to know dances that are hundreds of years old?" Briony asked with a smile.

"Hardly. I was only turned a month or so back, remember? So unless the gavotte is a vampire power people don't talk about much, I'm stuck with what I knew before." Fallon thought for a moment. "Which isn't much, when it comes to dancing."

That at least turned out to be a lie, because Fallon danced at least as well as Briony did, seeming to catch the rhythm of the music and let it flow through him as he moved. Briony did her best to keep up, and despite her great aunt's shoes, she felt she did quite well. They moved together, and Briony found that she could almost forget for a moment what Fallon was, what was going on in this strange little town.

Almost, but not completely. The slower dances were the worst part. Other couples pressed together tightly, close enough that it was often hard to see where one began and the other ended. Pepper's partner was certainly enjoying it. Briony and Fallon, on the other hand, found themselves further apart, hardly touching when they should have been close, stiffly formal when they should have been at their most natural.

The strangest part was that it wasn't even Briony doing it. There should probably have been some part of her reminding her of just how unnatural Fallon was, but for the moment she just wanted to forget that. She didn't want to spend the dance with the vampire who had admitted to hungering after her. She wanted to spend it with Fallon, who liked her when almost no one else did and who swapped critiques of odd sci-fi programs with her friends.

The trouble was that every time Briony tried to move closer, Fallon edged back. Was it the cross? No, that was safely hidden in the folds of Briony's dress. So it had to be something else. His hunger then? Was he really afraid of being that close to her? Briony considered simply kissing him, there and then, right in the middle of the dance floor. Maybe that would get across to him how she felt.

She didn't do it though. Instead, after a while, Briony excused herself and headed for the bathrooms. Maisy was already there.

"Wow," she said, "that dress looks even better tonight than it did in the store."

"Thanks. You're looking happy."

"Oh, I am! Steve finally got the hint and kissed me. It was wonderful, Briony…"

The next five minutes filled themselves with talk of Maisy and her boyfriend. Somehow, it made Briony feel better. She practically bounced back out onto the dance floor, finding Fallon off to one side and taking his wrist firmly.

"Now, you're either going to dance with me properly, or we might as well go home now."

For a moment, just a moment, Briony actually thought he might go for the second option. Then though, another slow dance began, and Briony pulled him close.

"There, that's not so bad, is it?"

"Bad isn't exactly the word I'd choose, no," Fallon admitted.

"Then shut up and dance with me."

Fallon did, and Briony reveled in the feeling of him pressed close to her now as they moved to the music. Before, Fallon had been elegant, cool, and distant. Somebody to watch, but something separate. Now, it was like he was a part of Briony, or rather like the two of them were one being, drifting through the crowd of other dancers to a single beat.

How long that continued for, Briony didn't know. Song followed song, and the two of them never seemed to break apart. Over Fallon's shoulder, Briony saw some of the other dancers staring at them. She also saw Pepper taking in the attention that was being directed their way, her expression growing steadily frostier.

Right then, Briony didn't care. The world containing Pepper Freeman existed somewhere else. Somewhere where she wasn't busy reading every movement of Fallon's body as they glided to the pulsing beat. Somewhere where time actually existed, rather than being something you ignored in the race to drink in *this* moment, *this* instant of perfect closeness.

Of course, it couldn't last forever. Nothing did, and Aunt Sophie had been perfectly clear when it came to her curfew. It was Fallon who pulled back, looking at his watch and declaring that he should get Briony home if he didn't want any elderly relatives coming after him. He wasn't entirely joking.

The drive back held a more comfortable kind of silence than the earlier one. Fallon kept glancing across to Briony, while she couldn't stop the satisfied smile that crept its way onto her lips and stayed there right up to the point when they pulled into the Edge Inn's driveway. With the car stopped, the two of them stopped too, just staring.

Briony wasn't sure which of them started the kiss. It felt more like something that both of them had known would happen, like a moment when they were only playing out roles scripted well in advance. It started as the barest brush of lips, but it built. It definitely built. Briony kissed Fallon with all the passion she could muster, and in return he covered her with kisses, his fingers entwining with hers, and his body pressed down on hers. He groaned while he buried his face into her hair and kissed his way down her face.

Her lips, the line of her jaw, her throat…

Fallon pulled back so suddenly, Briony knew there was something wrong even before she saw his fangs protruding. His hands, which had just a second ago been running across her shoulders, tightened on them almost painfully.

"Your lips taste so good. So perfect. I can almost taste your blood, Briony."

Briony tried to think of her options. The silver cross was still in her evening bag. She was too close to have a chance of kicking out with her stake-heeled shoes. Even getting to the small cross that hung around her neck would be difficult with Fallon gripping her arms.

"Fallon," she tried, "don't do this."

Wicked Woods

Fallon's face twisted into pain, anguish. "I don't think... I can stop. I need you, Briony. Please." His fangs edged towards her neck.

"No, Fallon."

"I know I shouldn't, but this hunger, this thirst is so strong." He turned his head away briefly. When he turned back to look at her, his eyes had glazed over with hunger, trained on her neck. "It wouldn't hurt. Not really. I could make it feel wonderful."

"I said no. You need to stop, Fallon. You're scaring me."

"Briony..."

"You gave me a cross to keep me safe. Is this keeping me safe?"

Fallon paused. Briony could see the need in his eyes. The hurt. Unfortunately, those eyes were also starting to glow red, so she wasn't really in the mood to pay attention.

"Let go of me Fallon. Right now."

Fallon hardly hesitated. "Oh God! Briony, I'm sorry. So sorry..." For all his hunger, for all that he had hardly been a vampire long enough to fight it, he did as she asked. He did more than that. Almost faster than Briony could follow, he was out of the car. A second later, and he was running for the forest. Briony started to get out of the car, stopped, and paused long enough to get the silver cross out of her evening bag. She stood there, on the drive, until her aunt came out of the house for her, a long knife not quite out of sight against her robe.

"Where's Fallon?" she asked.

Briony just shook her head.

Chapter 14

There was no sign of Fallon at school the next day. Briony had half expected it, and so, she suspected, had Aunt Sophie. At least, Aunt Sophie hadn't bothered giving her any advice on getting away with staking Fallon on school premises. To say that her great aunt wasn't happy with the vampire was an understatement. Only the fact that he had managed to stop short of actually biting Briony kept her from heading out with all the other members of the preservation society and hunting for him.

Briony's feelings were a lot less clear-cut. Yes, Fallon had been close to biting her, but he hadn't. He'd stopped in time, and she hadn't even had to hurt him. More than that, before it happened, everything had been going well. So well that she couldn't help wondering if one small bite would really matter that much. After all, people gave blood every day. Not that she was ever stupid enough to mention the thought in front of Aunt Sophie, or anyone else for that matter. Briony didn't even dare to say that what she really wanted was to see Fallon again long enough for them to talk this through. Talking, apparently, wasn't something you did with vampires when you could be busy staking them. As far as her great aunt was concerned, Fallon's incidence with Briony had only proven that.

School wasn't the same without him there. Maisy and Steve were still around, but in the couple of days after the dance they only had eyes for each other. As for everyone else, while they were mostly content to ignore Briony, some of them muttered behind her back about Fallon's sudden absence. Since the last time they had been seen together was at the dance, people seemed to be assuming that Briony had done something to upset him, to drive him away. If they only knew.

The thought of telling everyone the truth amused Briony for about five minutes. How would people react if she told them what had really happened? How would she even put it? "Oh yes, Fallon and I broke up because he's a vampire who tried to bite me" would probably get her laughed at, or even sent to have her head examined. It certainly wouldn't do anything to dispel her image as the strange girl of the class. Like it or not, though, Briony had to admit she missed Fallon a lot.

- 151 -

Wicked Woods

Her work at the diner proved to be a safe haven. There was something reliable about it, unchanging. Maybe that was even what Aunt Sophie had in mind when she suggested it, given how strange everything else in Briony's life was getting. Burgers didn't let you down. Fries didn't agonize over whether they were going to bite you. Side orders didn't avoid you, unless Percy had accidentally moved them when he shouldn't.

So Briony threw herself into her work. She showed up early for her next couple of shifts and stayed late afterwards. When she wasn't working, she spent her time training hard with Aunt Sophie, determined to get better when it came to fighting the things that showed up in the town. She asked questions of George and the others, hearing stories of even stranger and rarer things, from Wendigos to Ghouls, hiding out in the Wicked Woods. None of them sounded like Briony would want to meet them at any point soon.

It was on the third day that a familiar face showed up at the diner. Briony hadn't thought about Kevin since he had saved her. No, that wasn't true. She had thought about him, right up to the moment when Fallon had asked her out. After that though, thoughts of the handsome college guy who wasn't the hunter he had suggested he was had fled from her mind.

They came back now though, with him sitting at the same table he had occupied the first time, as though nothing had happened since. Briony's eyes narrowed at that. Did he really think that Briony was so stupid that she wouldn't have asked about him? Did he really believe that just being gorgeous was enough to let him waltz in here without a single explanation? Briony wasn't about to let him get away with that.

She took as many other orders as possible before getting around to his. Partly, it was to make him wait, because she was feeling at least a little bit petty today. Mostly though, it was because that would give Briony the time she needed to make this guy answer some questions. She ignored George's look over to her as she slid into the seat opposite Kevin.

"I might be remembering wrong," he said with a wink, "but I don't think this is supposed to be what happens when you take someone's order."

"Don't be smart," Briony snapped back.

Wicked Woods

Kevin raised an eyebrow. It was perfect, obviously. "And I'm almost *certain* that didn't happen last time either."

"No, but I can remember one or two things that did."

"Ah, so you're going to thank me. Well, if you have the sudden urge, you could always say it with extra fries."

He was, it seemed, determined to be infuriating. Briony decided to spell it out. It wasn't like anyone else who heard would care. The ones who knew were already in on the secret, while those who weren't would just ignore her. She was only a waitress, after all.

"You more or less told me that you were a hunter in my great aunt's society."

Kevin shook his head, causing his thick dark hair to fall over his face, his hazel eyes looking down and then directly at hers. Briony wondered if he was doing it deliberately, and then cursed herself for noticing at all. "No, I didn't."

"You did."

Kevin shook his head. "You assumed that. I hunt the things occasionally, but I'm not part of anyone's society. The whole idea of someone telling me what to do all the time..." he shuddered theatrically. "Although obviously, I'm big on the idea of telling other people what to do. Particularly if it means they might bring me food."

"In a minute," Briony said. "I just want to know what you're doing here. Don't tell me that it's a coincidence you're back in here."

"I'm hungry, this is a diner. It's kind of how these things work. Oh... you think I've come in just to see you?"

He said that in just the right tone to make Briony blush. She shook her head. "Stop it. Don't play games. Don't you think I have a right to find it odd when the mysterious guy who turned out not to be what I thought he was shows up where I work?"

Kevin paused. He licked his lips. "Not what you thought I was?"

"Not one of Aunt Sophie's society."

"Like I said, I don't like being told what to do. Besides, I don't like hanging around in one place that much. Mostly, I hunt on my own. I should probably have moved on from here by now, only..."

"Only?" Briony echoed.

Kevin grinned. "Well, it seems that there are one or two things worth hanging around for."

Wicked Woods

Was that a line? Of course it was. What kind of girl did he think she was? Him with his sudden appearances, and his casual flippancy, and his high cheekbones, muscles, beautiful eyes, great hair…

Briony stopped herself. She was *not* going to do this. Not when Fallon had just taken her heart on a roller coaster ride. Especially not given what she knew about Kevin already. He'd already told her that he moved around, so it wasn't like there was any chance of anything real, and as for dating college age guys… she could just guess what her great aunt would think of *that.* Or Briony supposed she could anyway. Knowing Aunt Sophie, of course, she would probably say something along the lines of "oh good, at least I don't have to stake this one."

"Not going to say something?" Kevin asked. A crowd started to come into the diner. Mostly kids Briony knew from the school. She ignored them for the moment, particularly since Pepper was among them, and would no doubt take great delight in bossing Briony around.

"What do you *want* me to say? You're not really going to tell me that you hung around just for me, are you?"

Kevin shrugged. "I keep my promises."

"And what is that supposed to-"

"Briony, customers." George's voice wasn't angry yet, but you could tell that he was used to people obeying orders. "You can gossip on your break."

Briony knew that Pepper would be smirking without even looking. Picking up her order pad, she stood to go over to her.

"Hey, don't I even get my food?" Kevin demanded.

"Maybe once you can give me a straight answer." Briony hurried off to do her job. George might be a friend of Aunt Sophie's and he might be a good employer, but if anything, those things just made it all the more important that she did her job well. Besides, the repairs to Aunt Sophie's car weren't paid for yet.

Pepper was everything that Briony had suspected that she would be. She ignored Briony as she approached the table. She kept her waiting while she poured over the menu, despite the fact that Briony could probably have told her what she would end up having. She waited until Briony had written her order down and then changed it. She made pointed comments about the wonderful time she'd had at the dance, and what a shame it was some people didn't seem to have had such a great evening. None of them were aimed at Briony directly, but they were definitely made with her in mind.

George only interfered once Briony had taken all the orders from that table, saying that he would take them their food. Presumably, leaving her alone for the first part of it had either been some kind of punishment for ignoring customers or George's idea of an important life lesson. Whichever it was, Briony was glad that it was over, even though he sent her on to the next table of customers rather than giving her the chance to talk to Kevin.

It was a busy evening. Half the school seemed to have come into the diner. It was good news for George, obviously, but it meant that Briony hardly had a moment to herself for the next hour. By the time the rush died down, Briony wasn't in any kind of mood to put up with backtalk from Kevin, and was determined that she would get some kind of answer out of him if it killed her.

That, however, proved a little awkward.

"George," Briony asked, "you haven't seen the guy I was talking to earlier?"

"What, the one who had you ignoring customers?"

"Sorry."

"He ate his burger and left twenty minutes ago," George said.

"And he didn't leave a message?"

"Should he have?" George paused, giving Briony a long look. "You're not in any trouble there, are you?"

Briony shrugged. "I really don't know. That's kind of the problem."

Chapter 15

When Briony got back from the diner, she was tired, and not entirely happy about Kevin's disappearing act, and irritable from having to put up with Pepper. The last thing she needed was more trouble. Unfortunately, Briony knew as well as anyone that trouble tended to hang around waiting for exactly the moment when you least wanted it before making itself known.

Aunt Sophie met her at the door to the Edge Inn. She looked grave, even by her usual standards, and Briony could see that she had something in her hand.

"What is it?" Briony asked.

Her great aunt held out a letter, unopened, with just "Briony" written in place of an address. "The vampire boy has been around."

Briony looked past her. There weren't any suspicious looking piles of dust lying around, were there? "You didn't... do anything, did you?"

"Well, I gave him a piece of my mind, certainly, but if you're asking whether I staked him, the answer is no. To be honest, my heart wasn't even in haranguing him. The boy looked upset enough as it was."

Briony let out a breath she hadn't realized she had been holding. Aunt Sophie gave her a sympathetic look. "He left this letter for you. I'm sorry."

"You've read it?" Briony demanded.

"No, but I can guess what is in it. Take it, Briony."

Now that Aunt Sophie had said it, Briony found that she could guess at one or two of the things that might be in the letter too. She took it anyway, heading up to her room with the envelope cradled in her fingers. There were times when you just needed to see things for yourself.

Briony waited until her bedroom door was firmly shut before ripping open the envelope. It held a faint, clear scent that reminded her of the way Fallon had smelled just before he had kissed her. Just the thought of that made something tighten in Briony's heart. Hardly daring to look, she took out the folded notepaper within and started to read.

Dear Briony, it read, *I know I am a coward to handle things like this, but I can't think what else to do. The homecoming dance proved that what I am counts for more than what I want, and if I stay around you, sooner or later I will end up hurting you. I cannot let myself do that. I will not let myself do that. I care too much for you.*

You will not see me again. I will not be returning to the school, and I will stay away from the inn. I can guess at how much that will hurt you. I can only say that it would hurt me more to see you dead. Goodbye.

I love you,

Fallon.

By the time Briony had finished reading, the first of her tears was ready to hit the page. It soaked through the thin paper, blurring the ink. Briony didn't care. In fact, she screwed up the note into a ball, flinging it as hard as she could at the opposite wall.

How could he do that? How could he just fling away everything they had in one moment? More than that, how could he *dare* to claim that he was just doing it for Briony's own good? He didn't want her hurt? Well what did Fallon think this was doing to her, because as far as Briony could tell, it hurt worse than practically anything? Somehow she felt hollow, as though her heart was wrenched away from her. She didn't realize it. She hadn't expected it. She loved Fallon.

More tears fell, and Briony didn't even try to stop them. She lay on the bed and sobbed until her throat was raw with it and her eyes were red. It wasn't just for Fallon. It was as though he had been the thing holding back the worst of the sadness that had been threatening to overwhelm her since her parents disappeared. It all rushed back now.

Briony remembered how bad things had been on those first days, and this was worse. It was like feeling the pain of her grief all over again, mixed in with the fresh pain of Fallon's abandonment, the loneliness of being the odd girl out at school, and the anger that came with Fallon making decisions like this for her.

How long she lay like that, Briony didn't know. She didn't care. As far as she was concerned, it didn't matter if she stayed there until the house decayed into a ruin around her. The rest of the world could go away. It wasn't full of anything but pain and strangeness, vampires and evil anyway.

Wicked Woods

The knock on the door came as a start, wakening Briony from the beginnings of a sleep she hadn't known she had been falling into. She winced at the sound.

"Go away."

"Briony." It was her great aunt. Of course it was. Who else would it be? No one else wanted her. Even Aunt Sophie only wanted her as her replacement. "Open the door please, dear."

Briony opened the door anyway. Aunt Sophie was standing there with a tray containing a bowl of soup and some crackers.

"I'm not hungry," Briony said.

Aunt Sophie raised an eyebrow. "Really? Well, I'll just put it by the side of the bed in case you change your mind." She put the soup down and then perched on the bed, patting the spot beside her. "Come and sit down, darling."

Briony did as she was told, letting herself be swept up in her great aunt's embrace. Aunt Sophie just held her like that for a long time, patting her cheek as she pulled back.

"It's going to be all right, Briony. I know it hurts now, but it will be all right. I promise."

"How would you know?" Briony demanded, and instantly felt contrite about doing so. "I'm sorry."

"I know. Besides, I'm hardly going to get angry with you, am I? You're all I have now."

"I'm your ticket to retirement, you mean," Briony said. "I know you don't really want me around."

"Oh, now you *are* making me just a little angry. You really think that's how I feel?"

Briony nodded. "I mean, why *would* you want me around? You're grieving for Uncle Pete, you have this place to run… I just get in the way and do stupid things like going on dates with vampires."

Aunt Sophie brushed a strand of hair out of Briony's eyes. "The only stupid thing you've done is to start talking like this, darling. You're my great niece, and I love you a great deal. Yes, it has been difficult losing Peter, but having you around has been nothing but a joy."

"Except for the car," Briony put it.

"Oh, that wasn't your fault. I only made you pay for it because I suspect I'm supposed to be teaching you responsibility. I was never much good at responsibility when I was your age. Now don't change the subject."

"Sorry."

Wicked Woods

Aunt Sophie sighed. "Briony, the point is that you have nothing to be sorry for. You're a wonderful young woman. You've been very brave since you got here, and no, I'm not talking about fighting monsters. I'm talking about the way you have dealt with things. You've lost so much, but you have still kept going. You have even found someone who cared about you, even if he does have one or two minor defects."

"Defects like the fangs and blood drinking?" Briony asked. "Or defects like dumping me just when I was starting to think…"

"That you love him?" Briony nodded silently. Aunt Sophie shrugged. "I was mostly thinking of the first defects, dear. After all, I'm looking after you. I'm not *meant* to like any of the boys you bring home." She paused. "He broke up with you, then?"

Briony nodded, curling up so that she could put her arms around her knees. "The worst part is that he says he's doing it for my own good. Like *this* is good."

"Yes," Aunt Sophie said, "young men can be very stupid about that kind of thing sometimes. He probably hasn't understood quite how much you love him."

Briony looked at her great aunt. "Why aren't you angry about that? I mean, he's a *vampire*. You hate vampires."

"I'm also old enough to know a thing or two about love, Briony." Aunt Sophie stood. "It's a tricky thing. It sneaks up on you. The more certain you are that it will never happen, the more it delights in proving you wrong. And of course, it has no sense whatsoever of how appropriate things might be. It just runs up, hits you, and leaves you to sort things out." She smiled. "It can be wonderful like that."

"But I shouldn't even *be* in love with him," Briony insisted. "There are so many problems, so many things that can go wrong. Maybe Fallon's right, and his leaving is for the best. It doesn't feel that way, though."

Aunt Sophie nodded. "I know. It feels like someone has replaced your heart with a rock. I'm glad you have realized just how hard this could be though. I'm glad your young vampire has too. Take it from me, Briony, falling in love with a vampire is easy. Staying that way, on the other hand, is one of the hardest things you can choose to do. All relationships with a vampire end in unhappiness eventually.

Wicked Woods

I would rather see you upset now, when you still have time to be happy again."

Briony nodded, even though she didn't really feel in that moment like things would ever be better. And although Aunt Sophie undoubtedly meant well, could she really understand what it was like?

Take it from me. Aunt Sophie had said almost as if... had *Aunt Sophie* once been in love with a vampire? No, she couldn't have been. She simply couldn't have been. Could she?

"Aunt Sophie-" Briony began, but her great aunt cut her off.

"I have things I should be getting to, darling, and I think you probably need to be on your own for a while. Please don't doubt for another moment though that I love you dearly. Oh, and don't let your soup get too cold. It never tastes very nice when that happens."

She was out of the door with the last words, and Briony didn't get the chance to finish her question. Somehow though, she suspected that there wouldn't be much point in going after Aunt Sophie now. There were moments when you could ask the big things, and Briony suspected that the moment for this one had passed. The most she would get out of Aunt Sophie now was a denial.

It didn't matter, because Briony suspected that she already knew the answer to her question. Knew it deep down, in her bones. At some point, Aunt Sophie *had* fallen in love with a vampire. And it hadn't ended well.

Chapter 16

Briony did not question Aunt Sophie about her past. There didn't seem to be much point, and in any case, she had to get to work at the diner. Briony thought about calling in and saying that she wasn't feeling up to it, but then she would have to explain why, and coming up with an explanation that didn't feature the words "my vampire boyfriend has dumped me" seemed like too much to bother with.

So instead, Briony spent her evening waiting on tables with a brisk efficiency and a forced smile that fooled nearly everyone, at least judging by the tips she received. At this rate, she would have the repairs to Aunt Sophie's car paid off in no time, not that she had any intention of quitting once they were.

Kevin came in, taking his usual seat and ordering the same burger and fries that he had ordered before. Briony wasn't in the mood to start a conversation from which he would just slip off, though, so she kept things professional, taking his order and making sure everybody else in the place was kept happy. After about five minutes, Jill the other waitress came up to her.

"Is everything ok?"

"Sure," Briony lied.

"If you say so, though I know an 'I'm going to keep working whatever' smile when I see one. I've worn a few in my time."

"I broke up with my boyfriend."

"Oh, honey, that's terrible." Jill treated her to a quick, one armed hug, made awkward both by the presence of a diner full of customers and by the fact that she was holding a hot coffee pot in the other hand. "Still, there's no shortage of potential replacements. The cute guy with the dark hair has been staring at you since he got in here."

"He's not interested in me that way," Briony said.

"Isn't he? Trust me, I've worked here long enough to know what I see."

Briony looked around for Kevin, deciding that this was something that needed to be sorted out before it went any further. Predictably enough, he was gone. What was it with him and running off? Did he think it made him seem more mysterious? Or had he just finished his burger? That was the problem with all this supernatural stuff. You could let it take over your thinking to the point where everything seemed bizarre and outlandish, and then you would find yourself forgetting that sometimes people did things for perfectly ordinary reasons.

Though not, Briony suspected, in Kevin's case.

Somehow she made it through her shift and back home to the Edge Inn. Home? When had it become home? Briony was too tired to think about it. Too tired to do much except finish her homework, watch a bit of TV with Aunt Sophie, and collapse into bed, asleep almost before she hit the pillow.

The next day brought more school, and with it, the stares of the other kids. Even Maisy and Steve looked at Briony for a long time as she arrived, though their expressions said that it was in sympathy rather than anything else. Maisy met Briony over by her locker.

"Are you okay?" she asked. "Only you look kind of upset."

"I'm fine," Briony lied. It was the kind of lie she was getting good at. After all, Maisy didn't want her misery sloshing over her, not when she was so happy with Steve now.

"I don't believe that for a minute. You are *so* not fine. Now come over and tell me and Steve all about it."

Maisy took a grip on Briony's arm that said quite clearly that she wasn't taking any nonsense from her, and more or less dragged her friend over to where Steve waited for them.

"Hi, Briony."

"Hi, Steve. Maisy, you can let go of my arm now."

Maisy shook her head. "Not until you tell me what is wrong. It's Fallon, isn't it?"

"Why do you think that?" Briony put it as carefully as she could.

"Well, he hasn't been in for a couple of days now."

"Maybe he's been sick," Briony suggested.

"Yeah, right. Now, are you going to tell me what happened? Did you guys fight or something?"

Briony found herself thinking back to the car. To the sight of Fallon's fangs glistening in the darkness.

"Or something. And then he broke up with me."

"That's terrible!"

Briony nodded. She knew that already. Knew it better than anyone. The three of them stood in uncomfortable silence for a few seconds.

Wicked Woods

"Look, Briony," Maisy said, "you know we like Fallon, he's a cool guy and everything, but he isn't the only boy out there."

Hadn't she had this conversation with Jill just the other night? It seemed strange to be getting the same advice from both her and Maisy, especially since as far as Briony could see, they were both wrong.

"He was the only one interested in me."

"Of course he isn't," Steve said. "Practically every boy in school would want a chance to... ow, Maisy!"

"Sorry, my elbow slipped."

"I said "practically". I didn't mean me."

"Of course you didn't," Maisy said, and grinned at Briony. "Steve has a point though. All the boys at school like you. It is one of the reasons Pepper hates you so much. In her world, they should all be lusting after her."

That was enough to make Briony smile in return, but she shook her head. "I think I am giving up on dating. It's not like I have time for it. I'm too busy working, most of the time."

Maisy rolled her eyes. "Oh come on! What kind of teenager are you? You've got to have at least *some* fun, you know."

Briony wasn't sure how that applied to her life, given everything else going on in it, but she promised that she would at least try. Mostly, she promised it so that Maisy wouldn't try anything silly like trying to set her up with someone. With a bit of effort, Briony managed to get through the day, and headed off to work as usual.

Kevin was there already when she showed up, and Briony felt her eyebrows rise as she passed his table.

"Two days in a row? That must be some kind of record for you."

"What can I say? I like the company here."

"Do you? It's not like you exactly stick about for it."

Kevin looked thoughtful for a moment. "Then maybe I should."

"I will believe that when I see it. Do you want the usual?"

Kevin nodded, and Briony hurried off to the kitchen to give his order to Pete. He was still there when she got back, which was a start at least. He was even still there twenty minutes later, having eaten the burger. Shouldn't he have run off by now?

Wicked Woods

In fact, Kevin stayed there for the next few hours, working his way through a succession of milkshakes as Briony kept up her service to the other customers. Whenever she looked over, his eyes were on her, and occasionally he would smile. It was almost disconcerting, having him sit there after the way he had just disappeared before.

Even George seemed to notice, asking Briony at one point if he was bothering her. Briony found herself shaking her head.

"No. He's actually kind of cute, doing this."

"Cute?" George gave her the look of someone who had never used the word before in his life. "If you say so. Just be careful. I mean, he's older than you."

"Only by two or three years."

"That's a long time, at your age." George paused. "Oh, would you listen to me? I'm turning into my old man."

Briony hugged him, which made George squirm uncomfortably. "And very grateful we all are too. I'll be careful, I promise."

"Sure you will. I'll tell you what, take out the trash and you can leave a little early tonight."

That struck Briony as a good deal, given that she took the trash out most nights anyway. She got the bags and hauled them out to the dumpster. By the time she got there, Kevin was leaning on it.

"You don't want to do that," Briony said. "You don't know what's in it."

"The same stuff that's in that bag, probably."

Briony winced and threw the thing into the dumpster. "How did you know I'd be back here?"

"I heard your boss say it. Would you maybe like to go somewhere after this?"

Briony had been half expecting it. "Um… maybe."

"There's something I would like to show you."

"Not the best line in the world," Briony observed.

Kevin shook his head. "Not really. Please? I think you'll like this, and you look like you could do with cheering up."

He had seen through the false smile? Most of the customers didn't look closely enough. For some reason, that made Briony feel happier than she had for most of the day. And Kevin had saved her life.

"Sure, I'll come with you. Um… after I've washed my hands."

Wicked Woods

It did not take long, and nor did the trip to the spot Kevin had in mind. They walked it, and as they did so, Briony found herself actually getting a feel for the town. Some towns needed to be walked around, it seemed. Their stroll ended at a small lake, built off to one side of the town square. Briony had passed it every day on her way to work, but had never really looked at it. There were ducks out on the water, along with the bigger shapes of swans.

"What are swans doing here?" Briony asked.

"It's home for them. Here, you'll see them better through these." Kevin passed her a small pair of binoculars. Obviously he had planned ahead. Through the binoculars, the swans were beautiful. They glided together in pairs, seeming almost to dance across the surface of the water. "They mate for life, you know."

"Really? I thought that was just something people said."

Kevin shook his head. "They mate for life, and wherever they find a mate, that's home. I guess for these swans, their hearts lie in Wicked."

Briony smiled at that. It was romantic, in a way. "How do you know all this, anyway?"

"I was going to become a veterinarian," Kevin said. "Hey, don't laugh. I was. At least until I showed up here with my brother."

"So what changed?" Briony asked.

"Everything. It all seems like a long time ago now, even though it's just a couple of months."

"I know what you mean," Briony said.

"I know you do." Kevin paused, staring out at the swans. "Briony, do you believe in destiny?"

Briony thought about it, and then nodded. "My great aunt tells me that it's my destiny to be here."

"She sounds like a wise woman. I don't. Or I didn't. Now though… oh, I'm not doing this right."

He kissed her then. It wasn't like the way Fallon had kissed her. There was nothing tentative about it. It was hard, passionate, and extremely good. It was all Briony could do to keep from melting under the intensity of it. When Kevin pulled back, she found herself gasping for breath.

"Meeting you felt like it was meant to happen, Briony. Like we were meant to… I'm getting this wrong again, aren't-"

Wicked Woods

Briony silenced him with a kiss of her own. She understood it. She didn't need the words. She could feel the attraction just as strongly as he did, and right then it was just enough to feel his arms around her, his lips on hers.

Chapter 17

It took Briony a few seconds to recognize the sound of her phone when it came, she was that caught up in the moment. Briefly, she considered ignoring it, but the ringing continued, and Briony knew she had to answer. After all, there weren't that many people who had her number, and Briony knew that most of them wouldn't call without a good reason.

It was Aunt Sophie. When Briony answered, her voice sounded tense.

"I need you to come back to the Inn, Briony. Something has happened."

"What?"

"Preservation Society business. Come back at once."

Briony hung up and then turned to Kevin. "I have to go. It is kind of urgent. Though maybe… would you like to help out? It sounds like an extra hunter could come in useful."

Kevin shook his head. "I am not sure that they would appreciate me just showing up. If you need extra help, I'll be around." Kevin kissed Briony again before they parted, cupping her face in his hand and looking earnestly into her eyes, "I'll definitely be around."

Briony jogged back to the diner, got in Aunt Sophie's car, and headed back to the Inn as quickly as she could. George's car was already there when she got there. He must have left in a hurry.

In fact, all the members of the diner's staff were there, along with half a dozen other people Briony didn't know. They sat in the Edge Inn's lounge, all clearly nervous. Aunt Sophie stood at the front. She looked up as Briony arrived.

"Good, we are all here. I won't waste your time with pleasantries. There has been a vampire attack. A fatal one."

Briony had been half-expecting some kind of collective gasp to go around the room, but everyone stared intensely straight at Aunt Sophie, expecting her to go on. "Do we know who?" Briony asked. A few of the society members looked over to her at that, like she shouldn't be interrupting.

Aunt Sophie nodded. "A girl from the local school by the name of Tracey Welston. I have a picture here somewhere."

Until she raised the photograph, Briony didn't get it. Even then, it was hard to connect the features of the dead girl in it to someone she knew, but once she did…

"Tracey? Tracey's *dead*?"

That got another disapproving look from a couple of the strangers there, but an interested one from her great aunt.

"You knew her?"

"She was my friend. Well, kind of. We would hang out when Pepper wasn't around. She was one of the girls who invited me to the football game."

Briony said it flatly, still hardly able to believe it. She had spoken to Tracey just… well, probably more than a couple of days ago, because Pepper had been hanging around a lot, and Tracey tended to be a bit more careful about that kind of thing than Claire, but not that long ago, anyway. How could she just be dead?

"Do her family know?" Briony asked.

Wicked Woods

"Not yet," one of the society members said. "For now, they just think she is missing. We will make it look like it was an accident. It's better that way."

Some accident. Briony could not help wondering what it was about her that meant things happened to the people around her. Her family had died, and Tracey had died, and Fallon had turned out to be... An awful thought struck Briony. Had Fallon been involved? She didn't want to think so, didn't want to believe it for a moment, but what if he had? He had said himself that his control was not perfect.

"What happened?" Briony asked, not daring to ask what she really wanted to know. Aunt Sophie seemed to hear the unspoken question too, though.

"It was a group of vampires, dear. At least four of them. Probably more. To drink all of someone's blood in a single sitting takes several of the creatures."

She said it in such a matter of fact way. Like there wasn't one of Briony's friends lying dead. Like this was all just normal, somehow. Briony couldn't think like that, because she couldn't help thinking about how things would be at school now. How would Claire take the news? The two of them had been inseparable.

"What do we do now?" Briony asked.

"Are you sure she should be involved?" one of the others asked. "She's not even fully trained."

Briony turned a glare on him that she hadn't known she possessed. "I'll stop being involved when people around me stop dying."

Aunt Sophie nodded. "Well said. Split into the usual pairings for the hunt. George, will you partner with my niece?"

The former soldier nodded. "Gladly."

They didn't rush out after that. Presumably, things did not end well when you rushed after vampires with no preparation. Instead, they went over the likely areas of the wood the vampires might be in, acquired weapons, and went over the importance of keeping in contact. Only after that did they trail off into the growing darkness together, flashlights and stakes ready.

George moved through the forest smoothly, with the care of someone who was obviously used to it, and Briony found herself wondering what kind of things he had done in the army. Except for the light beaming from their flashlight, the forest was pitch black, the air heavy like molasses. Briony scrambled after George, holding a short sword. Being a surer shot than Briony, the former soldier had a crossbow slung over his shoulder.

"Where are we?" Briony whispered to him

George put his finger to his lips. "Don't talk unless you have to. We need to listen. Vampires can move very-"

He spun and fired at a shape in the darkness. Briony was about to ask what he was doing, but then she saw the shadows gathering in the trees. They were under attack!

Briony brought up her short sword in time to plunge it through a vampire's shoulder, but that just made it scream and pull back. She slashed at another, looking for an opening that would let her thrust to the heart. How many of them were there? Briony could not tell in the darkness. All she could do was hear the quick swoosh of the air of approaching vampires gathering around them. It went on all around them, surrounding George and her. So many of them, getting closer and closer.

George shot up a flare, creating enough light for Briony to make out all the vampires surrounding them. And then, the one vampire Briony had been hoping not to see was there.

"Fallon…"

Briony had barely breathed the word before he was beside her, twisting Briony's arm behind her back hard enough that she yelped and dropped the blade. Briony could see a pair of vampires pinning George, a third tying his hands.

"Don't struggle, little vampire slayer," Fallon said, loud enough that the other vampires laughed at it. "I'll only hurt you if you do."

Briony started to drive an elbow back, but Fallon caught it, holding her while another of the vampires tied her wrists.

"Why, Fallon?" she demanded.

"Why not? After all, if I can't control my instincts, I might as well give into them."

"You know this human, Fallon?" Another of the vampires, a girl who didn't look any older than Briony, asked.

"I've been toying with her a little, Lily, yes."

It hurt to hear him put it so bluntly. Toying with her? Had that been all it had been to him?

"Well then, let's toy with her some more, shall we?" Lily suggested, grinning and coming over to seductively place a hand on Fallon's arm.

Wicked Woods

"Like you did with Tracey, you mean?" Briony shot back. She glared at Fallon. "Like *you* did?"

"Oh, Fallon didn't arrive in time for that one," the female vampire said. "Still, he's here now."

"Our master is not, though," Fallon said. "He will be angry if we don't let him know. I'll go and tell him."

Lily shook her head. "No, let the others go. You can stay here and get reacquainted with your little pet."

"I'm staying too," another of the vampires said gruffly. It was the one Briony had stabbed in the shoulder. He licked his fangs. "I owe her."

Briony saw the look the vampire gave her, raking his red-hot eyes over her from head to toe. She felt dirty, shuddering at the pure evil waiting to lunge at her. The other vampires scattered according to some unseen plan, leaving Briony and George alone with him, Lily, and Fallon. Lily ran her hand along Fallon's shoulder.

"What shall we play then?"

"Oh, all kinds of things," Fallon said. He stalked towards Briony.

"Keep away from me!"

"No." Fallon smirked as he said it, pressing her back against a tree. His beautiful blue eyes bore into hers.

Briony's eyes filled with unshed tears. Was Fallon going to kill her after everything? How stupid of her to have trusted him enough to love him before. Aunt Sophie was right…a romantic relationship between a vampire and a slayer would always end badly. His mouth opened, giving her an impressive view of his fangs. His mouth went to her neck… Briony closed her eyes, hoping that if Fallon was going to kill her, he'd be quick.

He placed the gentlest of kisses on Briony's throat as his hands went behind her, snapping the rope holding her with ease. His hands kept hers pressed there for a moment, until Briony got the message.

"Oh, you are a tease, Fallon," Lily said. "Making the poor thing wait like that."

"Perhaps you would like to begin things then?" Fallon suggested.

Lily brushed past him. "Nothing too damaging, of course. Just a taste." She moved close to Briony, but Briony wasn't watching. Instead, she was focused on Fallon as he picked up Briony's fallen sword in one movement, spinning towards the third vampire, the male she had stabbed.

Wicked Woods

"What?" was all the vampire had time for before the sword plunged under his ribs, up and into the heart. He fell back, cold flames already claiming him as he died. A second or two more, and there was nothing left of him.

Fallon lunged for Lily, but the female vampire was already reacting. She spun out of the way of the blow, kicking out at Fallon and catching him in the knee. He did not fall, but he did have to scramble back. Apparently from nowhere, Lily acquired a couple of wicked looking knives.

"Oh, how sweet. Trying to protect your little human. It will not work though. I am older than you are, Fallon, and we both know what that means, don't we? *Don't* we?"

"It means you are stronger and faster," Fallon said. He still raised the sword, circling until he was facing Briony. Or, to look at it another way, until the other vampire's back was to her.

"That's right," Lily said. "Don't worry though, I'm not going to kill you. Only the Master gets to do that. Besides, I'll want you alive while I hurt this human of yours so much that you *beg* me to kill...oh."

The last sound came out as a gasp. Briony had slid the crucifix from around her neck, activated the long blade, and slid it up into the spot where she thought the heart was. Since Lily flamed with that cold fire, Briony guessed that she had hit the right spot.

"That's for Tracey."

Somehow though, it didn't feel very satisfying. It certainly didn't do anything to bring her friend back. All Briony could do was move over and cut George's bindings. The ex-soldier looked over to Fallon and started to scramble for his crossbow.

"You won't need that," Briony said.

George paused for a moment. "How do we know?" He eyed Fallon critically.

Fallon walked over to Briony, slipping his arm around her, holding her close. "Because, sir, I love Briony. I would never do anything to harm her."

Briony's heart swell, hearing Fallon's words. Looking at Fallon's handsome face, full of love and earnestness, Briony wanted to lean into him and just let Fallon hold her. Fallon looked down at her, his cheeks brushing hers. "Briony…I'm sorry for leaving. I miss you."

"I missed you, too," Briony whispered, all her feelings for Fallon rushing back into her with full intensity.

Wicked Woods

George's gruff voice penetrated the thick air of passion between the two, and Briony instinctively pulled away from Fallon. "I believe you, vampire, although I'm not sure how a slayer could be dating a vampire." He addressed Briony, "Does Sophie know?"

Briony nodded.

"And she's fine with it?" George asked in disbelief.

"She allowed us to go to the dance together," Briony said.

"Well...you're her niece. She's very protective of you so if she trusts this vampire around you, then he is probably alright." George scratched his head. "What I do know about Sophie is, after all these years, that if she thinks someone is alright. She's usually right." George extended his hand. "Thanks...Fallon, is it? Your tactic was clever and fast-thinking." Fallon shook his hand.

"To be honest, I didn't really think it through." He reversed Briony's sword, passing it back to her. Briony accepted it gratefully.

"Well, I *have* been doing some thinking," George said, "and I think it's probably time for what we in army circles call a tactical withdrawal."

Fallon nodded. "They'll be here very soon…the rest of them."

George nodded. "And we don't want to be here when they come back."

Chapter 18

They scrambled back to the Edge Inn, all three of them, glancing back as they ran to check that the shadows between the trees were still just shadows, and not a horde of vampires about to descend on them. They stayed just as they were though. It seemed that the vampires had done enough with them for one night. At least, Briony hoped so.

There were still surprises in store though. No sooner had they reached the safe, comforting presence of the Inn than two shapes barreled out of the darkness at them. George raised his crossbow. Even Briony had her sword half up before she saw who it was.

"George, don't shoot. Maisy? Steve? What are *you* doing here?"

The two of them were warmly wrapped up, carrying torches and maps. Maisy spoke.

"We heard that Tracey had gone missing, and... well, we know she is your friend, and we wanted to help look for her. Um… if I ask what all the weapons are about, am I going to like the answer?"

Briony didn't get a chance to reply, because another shape detached itself from the darkness. It was a man in his twenties, his skin pallid, his eyes already glowing red in the dark. Another vampire then. Briony raised her sword again.

"You won't need that," the man said.

"I doubt that," Briony replied.

"I simply have a message."

"What kind of message?"

"A message for Fallon here, and a message for you." The vampire turned to Fallon. "We saw what you did to the others, traitor. Slaying your own kind. Our master has cast you out for that. Any of us who sees you has the right to your blood."

The vampire stopped for a second.

"What was the message for me?"

The vampire smiled eerily before lunging for Briony at a frightening speed. Unfortunately for the creature, Briony reacted on instinct, thrusting with the blade straight into its heart. The body fell and burned to ashes. Briony let out a deep breath. That was that then. All dealt with. Except…

Wicked Woods

Except that Maisy and Steve were watching from just a few feet away, shocked expressions on their faces.

"Um..." Briony tried to think of a lie that might work, decided that there probably wasn't one, and decided to try the truth instead. She looked to George, who shrugged. Apparently, this was going to be up to her. "I think I should probably explain a few things."

"I think you probably should," Maisy agreed, Steve leaning heavily on her. "Just help me get Steve inside first. I think he's fainted."

As it happened, Steve recovered quickly enough that Briony didn't have to help haul him inside, because he was able to walk. What he was not able to do was stop staring at the sword Briony held. Eventually, out of sheer irritation, Briony settled for tucking it out of sight under the sofa.

After that, while George watched from the windows for signs of the others, Briony did her best to explain. She explained about vampires. She explained about werewolves. She explained, in great detail, all the strange things that had happened to her since she showed up in the town of Wicked. Briony even explained some of the ways of killing vampires, mostly because the other two looked like they needed the extra reassurance that they could be killed. Finally, Briony explained about the preservation society, and what it did.

"So Tracey has been killed by a vampire?" Maisy asked.

Briony nodded. "A group of vampires, yes."

"And we can't tell anyone this because...?" Steve began.

Maisy punched him on the arm. "Because no one would believe us, idiot. They would think we were making things up, or insane. Or maybe they would think that we had something to do with killing her."

"You mean like in season three of *Vampires in Space?*"

"You mean season two, don't you?"

Steve looked sullen. "I do not."

"Actually," Fallon put in. "I'm fairly sure that it *was* season two, but that's not the point."

"No," Maisy said. "We get that."

Briony was impressed. "You're taking this a lot better than I did."

Maisy shrugged. "Well, we are confirmed sci-fi geeks, remember. All this stuff being out there... it is actually kind of cool. So, where do we sign up for this society of yours?"

That took Briony a little by surprise. "You want to join?"

"Of course we want to join! Out there, fighting against the forces of darkness! Who wouldn't want to? It will be so epic, won't it Steve?"

The boy nodded so vigorously, Briony thought his head might drop off. "Totally. I mean... *vampires?* Ok, so they might have been done to death on TV, but an actual society dedicated to fighting them? This is going to be amazing!"

"I don't think you two get it," Briony said. "This isn't a TV show. It is real life. You can really be hurt, out here."

Maisy nodded. "We know, Briony. But you haven't been, have you? Besides, after what they did to Tracey, I don't think hanging around pretending that nothing is happening here is going to keep us very safe."

Briony nodded. That made sense. "There are still things you need to see."

"Like?" Maisy asked.

Briony nodded to Fallon, who opened his mouth, revealing fangs. Briony wasn't sure what reaction she was expecting from her friends. Shock, maybe. Disbelief? Not for Maisy to lean forward, peering into Fallon's mouth like a particularly overeager dentist.

"That is *so* cool. Where do the fangs go when they are not out like this? I mean, do they retract, or do they just appear by magic, or what?"

Steve got in on the act. "So you're a vampire? Does this mean you're stronger than the whole football team put together? Do ordinary weapons bounce off you? What about sunlight? No, that can't hurt you. I've seen you walking around in the day."

Slowly though, the two ground to a halt. Maisy raised her hand like she was in class.

"What is it, Maisy?" Briony asked.

"Well, we're meant to be part of a society for hunting vampires, right?"

"Not until after I've spoken to Aunt Sophie about it," Briony said, but when she looked over to George, he nodded. "But yes."

"And Fallon is a vampire?"

"I am," Fallon said.

"So shouldn't we...be trying to stake you, or something? No offence."

"That," Aunt Sophie said from the doorway, "is where things get a little complicated."

Briony jerked around. Aunt Sophie had Jill with her. It could have been worse. Almost any of the other members of the society, for a start. Briony decided to make some introductions quickly.

"Aunt Sophie, you have met Maisy, and this is Steve, her boyfriend. They kind of... showed up."

"Ah," her great aunt said, "yes, that can be awkward. And they want to join the society?"

Briony nodded.

"Yes," Aunt Sophie said, "people sometimes do. Maisy, Steve? I think it is probably time that you went home, dears. We'll talk more tomorrow."

The pair looked at one another and then hurried from the Edge Inn. Aunt Sophie turned her attention to Fallon.

"I see you are back, young... man."

"Yes, Mrs. Edge."

George moved closer to Aunt Sophie, whispering to her. "And George here tells me that you saved both him and my niece."

"Yes, ma'am."

"Well then. I suppose that earns you something. You are welcome here, until you do something to make yourself unwelcome. Run along now too though. You probably won't want to be here once my colleagues show up."

Fallon hurried from the room without so much as a backward glance. Briony found herself faintly disappointed by that. Could he really leave that quickly, without even saying goodbye to her? Briony supposed that it probably had something to do with the fact that various vampire hunters were going to start showing up again soon, but even so, would a quick "bye, Briony" be too much to ask? Was Fallon still convinced that he could not be around her? Or maybe he blamed her for costing him his place in the vampire world. Briony had heard the threat to him as well as anyone.

For a while though, Briony had to forget about it as the various members of the preservation society wandered back in, coming back in the pairs they had left in, looking tired, bedraggled, and serious.

One by one, they recounted what they had found in the woods. Almost none of the others had run into anything but shadows and distant noises. The vampires had been there, but they had been playing games. Taunting the hunters and moving on. Or, to look at it another way, distracting them enough that they could attack Briony and George without opposition. The only other pair that had come under any kind of attack had been the one consisting of Jill and Aunt Sophie, and they had dealt with a trio of vampires easily enough, killing one before driving the others away.

It left Briony wondering why those two pairs had been the ones targeted. Presumably, the vampires could have attacked any of the others, but they chose not to. Something was definitely going on. The trouble was, she did not know what. Nor, from the looks of it, did anyone else. It wasn't a comfortable thought.

Eventually, the others left, getting rides with one another or driving off alone into the dark, leaving Briony alone with Aunt Sophie.

"I think what we both need," her great aunt declared, "is a late supper. Cheese on toast, I think."

She hurried off to the kitchen to make it, and at that moment, someone knocked on the door. Briony, remembering the first time she had gone to the door at night, wasn't exactly eager to go, but she had her cross, and the sword, and Aunt Sophie *was* busy. With an almost infinite degree of caution, Briony went to the door and pulled it open.

Fallon stood there, a bunch of flowers held out to her. They were an odd mixture, not roses or anything else Briony might have thought of as normal for a bouquet, but stranger flowers, night flowers. They weren't exactly pretty, but somehow, they were *right*.

"Fallon? What are you doing back here?"

He kissed her without a word, and it was a good kiss. It was sweet, delicate, almost… apologetic. Somehow, Briony knew that this was his way of saying sorry for everything that had happened. His way of telling her how much he still wanted her. When Fallon finally pulled back, sprinting off into the night again, Briony turned to see Aunt Sophie watching her.

"Complicated indeed."

Wicked Woods

That was more or less what Briony was thinking. Particularly since, now that the kiss was done, she found herself thinking of Kevin, and the way *he* had kissed her. At the time though, she hadn't thought of him at all.

Complicated. That was one way of putting it.

Chapter 19

Fallon was back at school the next day, as though nothing had happened. As far as the school was concerned, he had simply been ill for a few days and had to catch up on the work he had missed. Beyond that, hardly anyone remarked on his absence and return.

Mostly, that was because they were all too busy talking about what had happened to Tracey. The official story was that she had been walking in the woods, had tripped over, and had hit her head. If there were strange marks on her body, well... she had been walking through an area with a lot of thorn bushes. Of course she was going to have acquired one or two scratches and wounds as she fell.

Briony was hardly able to believe how easily people swallowed such a flimsy explanation. It said nothing about what Tracey was doing out there, and if people really couldn't tell the difference between fang marks and thorn scratches, they couldn't have been looking very hard at all.

Wicked Woods

It seemed almost like an insult to the other girl that people couldn't know the truth about her death.

They couldn't though, and that was that. Even though Claire was distraught at the loss of her best friend, crying in the hallway and hardly looking at anyone through lunch, even though a few people raised the thought that Tracey must have been up to no good to be out in the woods on her own, there simply wasn't any way that they would believe what had really happened.

It had to be enough that Briony knew the truth. Or rather, that Briony, Fallon, Maisy and Steve knew the truth. Briony had expected the latter two to be quiet today, as the implications of everything that had happened sank in. Instead, they seemed eager, asking Briony questions about the preservation society until she pointed out that it was really Aunt Sophie they should be asking, and that in any case, the middle of a busy school probably wasn't the best place to be talking about it.

Fallon was quieter, but his presence was a comfort. Just having him near made Briony feel safe, even if Fallon was now as much under threat from the vampires as she was. In class, she would seek him out, letting her hand slide into his when no one was looking, sitting close enough to feel him pressed against her when they were.

It drew stares from the people who had taunted her over what they thought had happened at the dance. No one commented, though. Today was about Tracey, and even the likes of Pepper knew that. Briony actually saw her trying to comfort Claire at one point. Briony took her own turn a little later, towards the end of lunch, when Claire was alone except for Ross. Claire looked up as Briony approached.

"Oh, Briony, did you hear about Tracey?"

"I heard," Briony said. A small wave of guilt pressed at her, but she ignored it. She wasn't the one who had hurt Tracey. She had just been the one to kill a couple of the vampires responsible. "I'm sorry. I know this must be hard."

"I don't know what I'm supposed to do now. I mean, she was always the brains. I... I'm just the stupid one."

"You're not stupid," Briony assured her, patting Claire's arm.

"Was it like this when your family..." Claire clearly couldn't bring herself to say the word.

"When they died," Briony said. She nodded.

Wicked Woods

"Only worse, probably," Claire guessed. "I'm being silly, aren't I? Crying like this when you've been so brave?" More tears started to fall.

"She was your friend," Briony said, not knowing what else to do. "You're entitled to be upset. If you need anything let me know, ok?"

Briony hurried out of there as quickly as she could. She felt sorry for Claire, she really did, but the last thing she needed was someone bringing back memories of her own losses. Especially with those losses being so recent. She sought out Fallon instead, eventually finding him in the school library, hunched over a book. It was the first time she had seen him quite that studious. Briony tiptoed forward as quietly as she could.

"Vampires have very good hearing, you know," Fallon said, without looking up. Briony sighed and settled into the chair next to him.

"I just saw Claire."

"It is harder for the people left behind, isn't it? And for you, being reminded, I'd guess." Fallon seemed to get these things at once. Briony liked that about him. Of course, he had his own losses.

"Yes," Briony admitted. "And it's hard having to lie to her."

"It's better than the truth."

"True. Still trying to catch up on your work?"

"A bit," Fallon said, looking up from his books. "I will be done soon though. Are you working at the diner today?"

Briony shook her head. "George decided that I deserved the night off. Jill's covering my shift."

"Well, can we maybe do something? You know, together?"

Briony cocked her head to one side. She had not expected Fallon ever to be that tongue-tied. It was kind of sweet. "You mean like a date?"

Fallon nodded. "Exactly like that. Very nearly, anyway."

"You have something in mind, don't you?"

"Let me drive you back from school and you'll find out."

Briony nodded. It was fine by her. Aunt Sophie had the car today anyway, because she needed to run errands. "I'll see you after school."

Wicked Woods

It proved to be a long wait. Time seemed to drag out deliberately until the bell, and even then, Briony thought that she might not be able to fight her way through the crush of leaving students. Finally though, she made it to the parking lot, where Fallon collected her in a roughed up SUV.

"It's hard to think of a vampire having a car," Briony said, as she got in.

"I nearly didn't," Fallon said, "except that this was going cheap. You know how vampires in the movies always have tons of cash for their castles and the rest of it? Not so true in real life…unless they've lived long enough to accumulate wealth and invest wisely."

Briony smiled at that. Would she have felt the same way about Fallon if he had been some super rich foreign count, born a hundred years before? It was impossible to know, though she suspected that the idea of going out with someone that much older than her, however young they looked, would have been a bit… creepy.

Fallon drove along happily, one of the local radio stations blasting out of the speakers as they headed back in the direction of the Edge Inn, and then beyond it, along the edge of the woods. He refused to say where they were going, except to say that Briony would see. Finally, he brought the SUV to a halt at the roadside.

"Come on," he said. "It's only a little way from here."

Briony followed eagerly. Fallon led the way down a little path to a spot where the trees cleared, and paused. It was perfect. A small stream bubbled through a meadow, and flowers surrounded it. Rocks in the stream made for a small weir, so that the water bubbled and frothed. The trees didn't resume at the far side, so that there was a clear view out over most of Wicked.

"I came here a few times with my brother to fish," Fallon explained. "I haven't been back since... that night, but I thought you would like it."

"It's beautiful," Briony said, and it was. She reached out to slip an arm around Fallon, and he held her, resting his chin on top of her head, gazing out with her over the pristine landscape. She snuggled up to him, feeling safe in his strong arms.

A landscape through which a familiar figure was approaching.

Briony tensed at the sight of Kevin. She had not seen him since she had kissed Fallon. She hadn't had a chance to talk to him. How angry would he be, seeing them here like this? She turned to Fallon to try and explain things, and saw that his expression was one of barely restrained fury. Did he already know?

"Fallon? What is it?"

"Kevin. My... brother."

The shock of that hit Briony, and not just at the thought that she had kissed both brothers without ever knowing who they were. There was also plenty of surprise at the way Fallon was reacting to the news that his brother was alive. Shouldn't he be *happy*?

Apparently not, judging by the way he stormed towards Kevin. The other young man didn't look any happier either.

"You're alive?" Fallon demanded. "I thought you were dead!"

Kevin paused a few strides away, nostrils flaring. "And you *are* dead, I see."

Briony hung back, not wanting to get in the way, even though there was a part of her that felt she should be trying to make this right.

"You didn't even look for me, did you?" Fallon demanded.

"Did you look for me?" Kevin shot back. "I wouldn't have been hard to find."

"I looked all over town!"

"When you weren't busy playing at being human."

Ah, Briony thought, that was it. Kevin was a hunter, after all. He wouldn't like the idea of a vampire for a brother. But if even Aunt Sophie could come around to the idea of Fallon, then he surely could. Fallon's expression twitched into a sneer.

"Not human? You think I can't smell what *you* are?"

"Then there's no point in hiding it, is there?"

One instant, Kevin was standing there. The next, there was the largest wolf Briony had seen. No *wonder* he hadn't been fazed by the sight of werewolves. And she had thought he hunted these things. At least, Briony hoped as the wolf let out a deep growl, she *hoped* that was all the hunting he did.

The worst part was that Fallon was falling into a fighting stance. Briony grabbed him by the shoulder.

"Fallon, what are you doing? He's your *brother*."

"He's a werewolf!" Fallon snapped back. His fangs were fully extended, his eyes red. He looked, if anything,

- 213 -

even worse than he had on the night of the homecoming dance. "He has to die."

"Why?" Briony demanded. She didn't quite step in front of Fallon. "Why does he have to die just because he isn't human anymore?"

"Not because of what he isn't. Because of what he is. Vampires and werewolves have hated each other forever."

Briony was going to ask why, but she didn't need to. She could imagine it for herself. Two predators, both hunting the same prey. Of course they would hate each other. It would be simple instinct. And little things like mere family ties wouldn't get in the way.

"Go!" Fallon ordered Briony, pushing her back. "Run! Once this begins, who knows if we will be able to stop?"

With that, he flung himself forward. The wolf that had been Kevin did the same. The two of them clashed together in a howling, snarling, biting whirl of flesh, each doing his level best to kill the other. All Briony could do was stare at it, trying helplessly to think of something she could do to stop the slaughter.

Briony took a deep breath, looking for a break in the violence. There was only one thing to do, even if it *was* stupid. The moment that there seemed to be space to do so, she threw herself forward, getting between Fallon and Kevin. For a moment, just for a moment, she suspected that she might have misjudged it. Fallon's eyes were a deep crimson as he started to swing a punch towards his brother. Kevin snapped and snarled. Briony forced herself not to move.

With a jerk, Fallon forced the strike aside before it could touch her. He tried to step to the side, around Briony. She stepped with him. Kevin tried to wheel around to the other side, but Briony stayed between them, keeping there in a careful dance of protection. Though who was going to protect her was anyone's guess.

"Stop this!" Briony ordered. The boys ignored her, continuing to circle and snarl. "You don't really want to kill each other."

"Oh, we do," Fallon said, "we definitely do. More than anything. It's instinct."

"Then fight the urge." Briony knew that she did not have long. Eventually, one of them would attack despite her presence, and then… well, they would probably all die. "Fight it, both of you."

"We can't!" Fallon looked anguished. "This is a part of what we are, Briony."

"Like trying to bite me was?"

"Yes!"

"But you fought that, Fallon. You didn't give in. You just have to be strong."

"This is *stronger*."

The wolf gave a snarl then. Briony guessed that Kevin agreed.

"Then I suppose Aunt Sophie is right. I can't trust you. If you cannot fight your instincts in this, then how will you fight them around me? There isn't any hope for us." She looked around to Kevin. "For any of us."

"This is what we have to do," Fallon insisted. "This is what we *are*. We cannot stop that, Briony. Please, just get out of the way before you get hurt."

"Before you hurt me, you mean. This is a choice, Fallon, your choice."

"Don't you see? There *is* no choice."

Briony shook her head. She didn't believe that. She wouldn't believe that. The moment she believed, it meant that Fallon and Kevin were nothing more than monsters, and that meant…

"You really believe that people are no more than that?" Briony demanded, pulling her cross pendant from around her neck and brandishing it. Fallon took a step back. "Well, I am supposed to be a hunter. I am supposed to kill vampires, Fallon. And werewolves. If none of us truly has a choice, then should I just give in to what I am supposed to be too? Should I kill the pair of you?"

Fallon didn't seem to have an answer to that. Nor, it seemed, did Kevin, who had changed back and stood glaring at his brother.

"I could move you out of the way," he said. "I'm not a vampire, I'm not afraid of crosses."

"This is silver," Briony pointed out. She activated the catch to let the blade spring free. "And so is this."

"You would really kill me to stop my brother from getting hurt?" Kevin demanded, looking hurt. "I thought you cared. I *know* you kissed me. Oh, didn't she tell you that, little brother? She kissed me too."

"If you try to move me, I won't be killing you for Fallon," Briony said. "I will be killing you because you will have become nothing more than a monster. If you can't control yourself that much, how could anyone be safe?"

Kevin fell silent at that, and so did Fallon, but it was a tense silence. They weren't trying to attack each other anymore, but that was simply because Briony was in the way. She knew just from looking at them that the moment she stepped back, one of them would attack the other. She simply didn't know what to do.

The faint sound of applause came to her, and Briony looked around. There were shapes in the trees, and more out across the meadow. At least a dozen of them. Probably more. What were they? Werewolves, vampires? It was too much to ask that they might be human. Far too much.

They started to step out from the shadows, one by one, taking their time. They clearly knew that there wasn't anywhere to run, and they were enjoying it. They were pale, and glorious, dressed in everything from clothes from the nineteenth century to the latest fashions, their eyes glowing red in the half-light. Many of them were Briony's age, while others looked a little older, in their twenties and thirties. Not one of them was anything less than beautiful. Vampires.

The applause continued, just slow enough to be sarcastic, but not coming from any of the vampires who had stepped forward so far. Those glanced nervously between Briony and a point she couldn't see in the trees. Whatever was going on then, it concerned her.

Finally, the sound gave way to that of a throaty chuckle. It wasn't a maniacal laugh, or a deranged titter, or any of the other out of control expressions of mirth Briony might have associated with villainy, but somehow, that amused little sound managed to convey a sense of evil in a way Briony wouldn't have thought possible. She really didn't want to meet that laugh's owner, which was a pity, because Briony suspected that in a moment or two, she was going to.

"Pietre," Fallon whispered, and Briony could hear the fear there.

At first glance, the man who stepped from the trees did not seem like he should have inspired such emotion. He was as good-looking as any of his flock, though perhaps a little older when he was transformed, looking forty when none of those around him got close to it. He was dressed in modern clothes, an expensive looking suit in dark gray that went well with his nicely-groomed pale blond hair. His shoes looked better suited to a sidewalk than to trampling through woodland. He looked, to Briony, like a fairly successful businessman or at least an older elegant European male model that just happened to have wandered into the middle of a group of vampires.

She went on thinking that right up to the point where he looked at her directly. Power rolled over her then. Power, and age, and the sense of something darker behind it. The sense of a life, not just infinitely prolonged, but utterly given over to evil. Briony could almost taste it, dull and metallic on her tongue. In that moment, she found herself in no doubt that this was the vampires' leader, the master.

"Well." His voice held just the faintest trace of an accent. Was it from some far off place, or just some far off time? "Finally, I get to meet you in the flesh. Sophie's young replacement. It is an honor, of course."

The mocking little smile that went with that told the truth about what he was feeling. Briony made sure that she kept the cross between them. It probably said a lot about how terrifying the new arrival was that even Fallon and Kevin had given up trying to kill one another for the time being, standing near one another, their eyes darting to the surrounding danger.

"I am Pietre," the master vampire said. "Could I persuade you to put that trinket down, Briony?"

He knew her name. Briony cursed herself for her stupidity. There were vampires in her school. Of course he knew her name. "No."

"Ah, of course. You think it will protect you. I will have to change your mind on that. But first..."

He moved as quickly as any vampire Briony had seen, stepping past her to Fallon and Kevin. In a second, he had a hand around each of their throats, and had lifted them clear off the ground. Kevin made a strangled sound.

"Strictly speaking," Pietre said, "Fallon here does not need to breathe. It is a habit. An affectation. One I gave up on long ago. On the other hand, a snapped neck will kill him as surely as any other vampire."

"What do you want?" Briony demanded, still keeping her cross up.

The vampire ignored her. "Heart and neck. I always tell them, guard your heart and neck, but do they listen? His heart... well, I think you have that, and now, thanks to

Fallon's efforts against his brethren, I will have his neck. As for the wolf, it's always nice to deal with vermin."

Briony saw his grip start to tighten. She had to think of something. "Wait," she tried. "Let them go and I'll... I'll let you do whatever you want with me."

That got another of those laughs. Briony hated him for that. Hated that anyone could behave like this and find it *amusing.*

"Oh, dear Briony. How very self-sacrificing. Haven't you worked it out yet? You are surrounded. Very soon, you will be captured. And then I get to do whatever I want with you anyway. At some considerable length. That these two will die is just a bonus."

That made Briony shudder. She did not want to think about what the vampire had in store for her. About what a mind like that might decide to do when it had her helpless. But she couldn't exactly fight her way free. Yes, she had her cross, but what happened when vampires rushed her from all sides? Besides, by that point, Fallon and Kevin would be dead. Briony wasn't sure that she could live with that. Yet what else could she do?

Slowly, Briony looked down at the cross. At its sharpened blade. She thought back to the way Pietre had looked at her as he entered the clearing. To the looks from the vampires. They wanted her for something. They needed her. Silently hoping that she was right, Briony lifted the blade to her own throat.

"Stop!" she ordered. "Stop, or whatever you want me for, you won't get the chance."

"You wouldn't dare," Pietre countered.

"Wouldn't I? You really think that death isn't better than what you have in store? You think I'll take that chance with Fallon and Kevin dead?"

Pietre appeared to consider it. "Put the knife down, you foolish girl."

"No. Not until you give me your word that you won't kill them."

"And then?"

Briony swallowed. It had to be this way. It had to. "And then I will come with you willingly."

The master vampire nodded, throwing the two boys down in a gasping heap.

"There."

Briony considered running for it then, but her chances of escape weren't any better than last time. Besides, what would stop Pietre from killing Fallon and

Kevin then? She squeezed her eyes shut and dropped the blade. Hands were on her instantly, grasping her arms, caressing her cheek. The voices of other vampires came to her then, whispering close.

"Open your eyes, little human. Open your eyes, Briony. It will be so much better. Open your eyes."

Pietre's voice cut through it. "Open your eyes, or I will change my mind, girl. I have my prize, after all."

Briony winced at that. She knew then that this was going to be worse than she could possibly have imagined. She opened her eyes, staring up into those of another of the vampires. Such beautiful eyes. Such beautiful...

Darkness claimed her.

Chapter 20

Briony came to sitting on a chair. It was a straight-backed wooden chair that was as far from comfortable as could be, particularly in comparison to the armchairs that filled the rest of the room. Those had a slightly frayed look, as though their glory days were long behind them, but at least they went with the rest of the décor in that respect. The whole place had a look of slightly tattered opulence, as though it had been a mansion at one point, but nobody had bothered with repairs for a few years.

Her lack of comfort was at least partly down to the fact that she was tied to the chair. Securely too, because straining against whatever ropes held her didn't result in any give. Another part of it had to do with the view. From where she sat, Briony could see out through the door to the room, across a corridor, and into the opposite room. That was bare, except for two solid looking chairs similar to hers. They held Fallon and Kevin, both tied, both bruised, and both currently unconscious. What did it take to knock a vampire and a werewolf out? Briony hoped that she would never find out.

As she watched, Pietre stepped out of that room and shut the door behind him. He was down to his shirtsleeves now, and there was blood on those. He stepped across to Briony in an unhurried fashion.

"And so you wake." He picked one of the armchairs and sat down. It was to Briony's side, so that she had to strain in her seat to see him. She knew without asking that it was deliberate.

"So what? Are you going to torture me now? And I thought Kevin and Fallon weren't going to be harmed."

"I said not killed," Pietre retorted. "I never said anything about leaving them alone. As for you, I am more inclined to talk right now. Harming you could cause problems. Unless you would rather I bit you?"

"Never."

"Really? Some people rather enjoy it. Some people practically beg for it. Feeders…for instance."

"Well, I'm not one of them," Briony snapped. "And I can't believe that *anyone* would willingly give themselves to you."

The master vampire stepped out of sight behind her, and for a moment, Briony suspected that she had made a serious mistake. Helpless as she was, could she really afford to anger someone that powerful? Would the next thing she felt, the last thing she felt, be his fangs at her throat? Or worse, would that only be the start? What had Aunt Sophie said back at the Inn? That it would take more than one bite to drain someone completely? Just the thought of it made Briony shiver.

"Hmm..." Pietre was right next to her. "So much fear. And yet... what if it were young Fallon offering to taste you? Would it be so terrifying? Or would there be a part of you that wanted it?"

Briony shook her head, not daring to speak.

"You know," the master vampire said, "I think you actually believe that. Suffice it to say that there are others who are more honest about their desires. There are those who will do almost anything for us."

"You really expect me to believe that there are humans out there who sympathize with you?" Briony asked.

"I do. You would know it, if you only stopped to think. People think we are exciting. That we are beautiful.

Wicked Woods

And so they help us. Either they do it for the pleasure, or from love of what we are, or the promise of what we can give them. Take this house. I would never have found it without the aid of a human or two. Though they didn't exactly get the reward they were looking for."

That made Briony look around the room again. Had this been someone's home? Had they invited the vampires into it, seduced by the promise of eternal youth, or by simpler things like money or pleasure? From the sounds of it, whatever they had wanted, they had found death instead. Briony couldn't help feeling sorry for them, whoever they were.

"Where are we, anyway?"

"Plotting your escape already?" Pietre asked. His hands moved to rest lightly on Briony's shoulders. "Perhaps you would like a map, a knife, and a running start?"

Briony forced herself to stay calm. "It might be an idea."

"Oh, I think I am going to like having you as my guest," the master vampire said. "As for where we are, let us simply say that you are deep enough in the woods that your screams will not be heard, and far enough from help that we could hunt you down before you got to it, were you to attempt an escape."

Briony could believe that. There were no sounds of traffic nearby, not even in the distance. Wherever they were, she was a long way from help.

"Nothing to say?" Pietre asked. "Or are you simply trying to be brave like your great aunt?"

"Leave Aunt Sophie out of this."

Pietre moved back round into view, crouching before Briony. "Why should I? Tell me, is she still as sympathetic to my kind as she used to be? I know she kills mostly werewolves."

Briony couldn't help laughing then. Just the thought that Aunt Sophie would *ever* sympathize with creatures like this was ludicrous. She laughed, and laughed, right up to the point where Pietre's fingers tightened around her throat.

"You do not like the thought? I assure you that it is true. I know from personal experience. Why, when we were both much younger, Sophie sympathized with me very much. *Very* much."

He let go of Briony then, and she gasped for breath. No, she wouldn't believe it. Aunt Sophie would never have... not with a monster like this.

Wicked Woods

"You can't bring yourself to believe it, can you?" Pietre said it gently, as though he hadn't just been choking her. "I understand, I really do. Yet my Sophie was very much in love with me, and I with her, truth be told. At least up until the day when she tried to drive a stake into me. Apparently, forever didn't appeal to her. Perhaps it will now."

Briony looked at him, so earnest as he crouched there, so deadly and so evil. She couldn't really imagine Aunt Sophie ever falling in love with something like this, though it certainly fit with some of the things she had said. Briony could certainly imagine her trying to kill him, though. Another thought came to her.

"Kidnapping me is just about Aunt Sophie, isn't it?"

"Kidnapping you?" Pietre laughed that nasty little laugh of his. "Oh, I have done far more than that to get her attention. Picking off her family, harrying the town. This is just the last act. Maybe finally, dear Sophie will come to me as she was always meant to. Begging. Of course, after her little rejection of me I vowed to kill her, so it won't make a great deal of difference, but she will come to me."

This was all down to that one moment? All of it? Her family's deaths? The attacks? All the misery that had seemed to surround Briony like a cloud? It had all been focused on Aunt Sophie? There seemed to be only one thing to say to that.

"You do realize that this makes you look like a total stalker, don't you? I mean, okay, it wasn't exactly a great break up, but don't you think all this is a bit... obsessive?"

That was the wrong thing to say, it seemed. With the sound of splintering wood, Briony found herself hauled from the chair and dragged, literally dragged, across the hall to the room where Fallon and Kevin were being held. They were awake by now, but still tied and gagged. Pietre tossed her to her knees before them.

"You think this is some joke? We will see how funny you find it, human. Now, you are going to help me to bring your great aunt here, doing whatever it takes to bring her to me."

Briony shook her head. "I will not. There's nothing that you can do that will make me betray her like that."

Pietre smiled, or at least, he peeled his lips back to reveal his fangs. "I was hoping you would say that. It occurs to me that, with two prisoners here, I have one more than I really need to keep you obedient."

Wicked Woods

It took a moment for the threat to sink in. Briony looked up at him, horrified. "No, you wouldn't-"

"Of course I would." The master vampire seemed to be enjoying it. "I would even enjoy it. And it would simplify things for you, of course." He moved to kneel beside her, wrapping an arm around Briony's waist and whispering in her ear. "Poor little thing, with two handsome brothers wanting her. *Such* a difficult choice to make. My heart goes out to you. Now, which one should I kill, Briony? Choose."

"No, please," Briony began. Pietre put a finger on her lips.

"Too late for that. It is time to choose now. No? Then I will. The werewolf first, I think."

He rose, standing behind Kevin and bunching his hand into the werewolf's hair to yank his throat into a taut line. His fangs came down, and Kevin gasped in pain. Even Fallon struggled against his bonds, trying desperately to get to his brother. The worst part, the very worst, was that Pietre kept his gaze on Briony the whole time that he was drinking.

"Please," Briony begged. She could feel the tears starting to fall. "I will do anything you want. Anything."

Pietre pulled away from Kevin, letting the young man fall limp in his chair. Briony could see the rise and fall of his chest. He was still breathing. That was something, at least. Pietre pulled her to her feet, forcing Briony from the room and slamming the door behind them. The last view Briony had was of Fallon looking forlornly over at his brother.

"You know," Pietre said, guiding Briony to one of the armchairs in the other room, "you are a very lucky young woman."

"Lucky. Right."

Pietre's eyes narrowed. "Lucky indeed. After all, it would be so easy to drink your blood instead of just your boyfriends'. To teach you obedience. But you are lucky enough that your family has become popular in my nest here, and news that you have been hurt would not go down well."

As shocked as she was by everything else, it took a moment for that to get through to Briony. "My family?"

Pietre smirked. "Oh, you didn't know? Vampires one and all now. I think that will hurt Sophie more than almost anything. Perhaps, in time, I will turn you too. Yes, that might be fun. For now though..."

Wicked Woods

He rose and left before Briony could respond. Though in truth she didn't know *how* to respond. Elation at the news that the members of her family weren't dead mixed with fury at what had been done to them, then despair at the thought of what might be to come. Briony lay on the armchair and cried unashamedly as the door slammed, leaving her utterly alone.

Wicked Woods continues in
Book 2 of Wicked Woods

Shimmer

Available Now

Kailin Gow

From Top Author for Young Adults
Kailin Gow

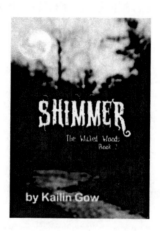

Shimmer (Wicked Woods, #2)

In the small charming resort town known as Wicked, MA, lies an age-old secret. Newcomer Briony Patterson, who has recently lost her parents and younger brother, will soon find out what it is...

Available NOW!

AN EXCERPT FROM DAUGHTERS OF DRACULA

(THE STOKER SISTERS, BOOK 1)

****

Prologue

ʃ

Dorset, England 1818

The sun was faint as it made its way through the veil of clouds that obscured the sky and shone down on Stoker Manor. Sadie's desire to keep her fair skin from being touched by the sun made these days the most enjoyable of all. The small bonnet she wore over her flaxen hair barely shielded her from its penetrating rays.

Seated near the garden she breathed in the pleasant saltiness of the ocean air as she threw herself in the Jane Austen novel she was reading. The young woman she'd met the year before in Bath had inspirational talent and Sadie held to the hope she could one day have the ability to write with such flourish, even if female authors were frowned upon.

"I'm feeling a bit chilled," Alexis complained as she set down her copy of the same novel. Always a little more daring in her attire, her shoulders were almost completely exposed. She'd even had the gumption to pull her skirt up well past her knee.

Sadie should have been mortified by such a scandalous act, but Alexis had always had a penchant for shocking people. Alexis, at nineteen, was older than Sadie less than two years, yet she was the sister whom their parents fraught over constantly.

"Perhaps a shawl would do the trick." Alexis stood and gazed out at the horizon. The ocean, with its ceaseless breeze, crashed on the beach below. "The cool air will only grow colder with the day."

Alexis turned to head towards the manor, but the moment Sadie noticed the young, handsome man approaching them, she knew Alexis would not be going anywhere.

With the charm and eloquence of a young lady about to be presented in society, Alexis curtsied, smiled and did all she could to capture the young man's interest.

"Terribly sorry to disturb you," he said, his blues eyes twinkling behind the black wave of hair that fell over them. "But I seem to have lost my way."

Alexis tossed her thick raven hair off her face and swayed her hips as she stepped closer to him. She was flushed, her smoldering dark eyes glittering with admiring excitement. "I'd be more than delighted to guide you to your destination, my kind sir."

"I'm searching for Stoker Manor. I've some pressing matters to tend to with the Mayor in town and was told I could find a room to stay."

A low rumble came from Alexis' throat as she chuckled, keeping a seductive eye on the startling blue of his. "How fortunate. Your search has come to an end."

Sadie watched her sister's antics with a blend of disdain and awe. The young man was clearly one of the most physically-gifted men the two sisters have laid eyes on. He was finely dressed in a silk and wool tailored coat, a brocade vest, and white silk shirt that opened a tad more than most men's shirts. His cream breeches filled out with muscular legs, legs that were used to physical exertion, but he held himself straight and tall, the posture of a noble-born. Sadie had never observed a man this closely, yet she could not take her eyes away from him.

"Splendid. I was indeed hoping I was at the right place." His eyes bore through Alexis' for an intense moment before he turned to greet Sadie. "This is even more enchanting than I'd imagined."

Sadie's heart fluttered under his gaze and her hands were instantly damp on the pages of her book. She set it down and rose to her feet.

"Will the mayor be meeting you here?" she asked, always eager to have men of influence visiting their humble manor.

"Perhaps." His smile held a touch of whimsy that didn't touch his eyes. A blend of austere businessman and boyish prankster seemed to lurk beneath the pristine veneer of his stylish clothing.

Perhaps more disturbing was the underlying streak of danger Sadie perceived. No doubt this was what had drawn Alexis to him so instantly.

"I'm to propose a building project for the neglected and vacant lot not too far from here. I believe this setting could do wonders in persuading him to see my vision."

"How impressive," Alexis purred. Despite the chill she'd complained about, she picked up her fan and swept cool air across her face. "I'm sure you could persuade virtually anyone into doing anything you desired."

Sadie wanted to die for witnessing such a brazen performance.

He smiled a slow smile before he replied. ""Well, I must be off." He removed his hat and nodded. "Ladies."

The moment he was out of earshot, Alexis giggled. "I don't remember ever meeting such a dashing young man."

"I do."

Alexis turned a skeptical glance at Sadie. "You lead a life that is far too sheltered to have ever met a young man at all, never mind one who is so worldly and witty."

Sadie picked up her book and held it up to Alexis. "Mr. Darcy."

"Why I do say, I believe you're right. He is Mr. Darcy come to life." She turned to the direction the young man had taken. "Could he be the very man who inspired our friend Jane so?"

"I seriously doubt it, but the resemblance is quite startling. My desire to read more is heightened."

"Oh, posh. Reading about such a fine specimen of a man is fine on a dull, dreary night alone. But when you have the real thing, heated and coursing with real blood staying under the very same roof, there is no longer a need to simply read about it." Alexis' eyes flashed with excitement.

"Alexis, he's to board with us. You know very well what Mother and Father say about interacting with the guests here."

"They say to be polite and engaging, and that is precisely what I intend to be, dear sister. You underestimate me." She ran her hand over her bonnet then passed it over the straight skirt of her simple frock. "I think I'll go inside to see if he needs assistance settling in."

"Not so fast, Alexis."

Both girls turned to the stern voice of their tutor, Delilah Wu.

"The only assistance you'll be tending to is on a canvas."

"Are we painting today, Miss Wu?" Sadie was quick to set her book down and show her enthusiasm for the day's art lesson. Her love of the fine arts had grown and her desire to put paint to canvas had intensified steadily with each lesson.

"Indeed we shall, Sadie."

"I believe tending to our guest is of more import than splattering paint on a canvas," Alexis argued.

"Your parents would disagree. Now let's get started before the scant daylight we have is further diminished."

Sadie tried to ignore the blatant manner in which her sister glared at Miss Wu. Though nearing thirty, Delilah had features that were both exotic and familiar. Her mass of black hair was pulled back into a tight chignon, foregoing ringlets that were the fashion of the day. This emphasized her fragile beauty all the more. While Alexis would never admit it, Sadie suspected there was a subtle sense of competition between the women.

"Could our subject be a handsome model?" Alexis asked.

Sadie knew exactly who Alexis wanted to immortalize on her canvas and had to admit the image of the handsome young man was still fresh and clear in her mind and would make for an exquisite portrait.

Miss Wu set her large carrying case on the table and pulled out an old leather bound book, ink well and quill, and pocket watch. Gazing at the sky to gauge the source of light, she adjusted the items on a small round table she'd covered with a yard of lace and turned to the girls.

Alexis quickly huffed. "You want us to paint those?"

"I want you to bring life to these items. I want light and shadow. I want depth and subtleties. I want texture and realism."

"Do you want to know what the book is about, while we're at it?"

"Alexis!"

"I'm sorry, but I'd rather paint anything than these dreary drab objects...for instance...handsome young men."

"The key is to find within you the life that these items should portray." Miss Wu turned to

Alexis. As usual she was completely unperturbed by the outburst. "If you have the passion, it should come through, no matter the item you're painting."

For the next hour the girls settled into the task of bringing passion and realism to their canvasses. Other than the sound of the crashing waves below, the garden was peaceful and quiet, rendering it all the more evident when Serene poked her canvas firmly with the bristles of her brush, stiffened her back and sat straight up.

A sidelong glance at Alexis confirmed what Sadie had perceived and before she could question the reason for the sudden change in her sister's stance and painting style, she heard the faint brush of footsteps on the lawn. Her heartbeat immediately sped up with anticipation.

She looked at her canvas, hoping it was suitably impressive then took a brief look at Alexis' ailing attempt. Pleased with herself, she nonetheless felt a pang of sympathy for the bleak effort her sister had brought to Miss Wu's vision of still life.

"Alexis. Sadie."

In unison, the girls turned to the sound of the crusty familiar voice. Their father, Edmund Stoker stood before them.

"I'd like to introduce you to Lord Ashwin. He's come all the way from Cambridge to enjoy the beautiful setting of our ocean side manor."

"Pleased to make your acquaintance, sir." Sadie bowed demurely and glanced up at the young man whose handsome visage had haunted her the entire day from under her lashes.

"As am I, Lord Ashwin." Alexis wasted no time approaching the young Lord. "I do hope you'll allow me to do what I can to make your stay here as pleasant and comfortable as I can."

Lord Ashwin glanced briefly at both ladies' faces before his gaze lingered down to their smooth lovely throats. "I most certainly shall."

Kailin Gow

ʃ

Praise for

Daughters of Dracula (The Stoker Sisters, #1)

"Is the ultimate vampire story! It's dangerous, dark and exciting!"

- Faye, *Ramblings of a Teenage Bookworm*

"Daughters of Dracula is a highly addictive novel that completely took me by surprise. With its references to Romanian mythology and Victorian society, readers are introduced to a completely different side of the typical Dracula vampire story. With Gow and her tale, everything seems more realistic... well, as realistic as it can get when you are discussing vampires. Sadie and Alexis are some of the best characters that I have seen in a while. And readers are sure to be picking sides in this sibling rivalry.

– Kate, *The Neverending Bookshelf*

Yet another amazing and perfect story from Kailin Gow! Okay, I am going to do a bit of gushing. I was first introduced to Kailin Gow's work with The Phantom Diaries, which I instantly fell in love with. I then went on to read Bitter Frost, which I greatly enjoyed and now with her newest series, The Stoker Sisters, Ms. Gow has won a place in my heart and library as one of my absolute favorite authors. Her ability to take a well-known classic story (in this case Bram Stoker's Dracula) and create an amazing story which includes bits and pieces of the original well-known stories, intertwining them with her own mind-blowing imagination and creating a "what-if" scenario that will leave the reader racing through pages to see what happens next, is magnificent.

– April Pohren, *Café of Dreams*

Kailin Gow

From Bestselling Author Kailin Gow

The Stoker Sisters

Two sisters... Born during the time of Jane Austen... Set to marry for advancement, but escaped their fates by becoming vampires. Now vampires in the 21st century, hunted by a sect of rogue hunters, the sisters meet a mysterious boy who holds the key to their destinies.

Now in development as a television series.

Want to Know More about the *Wicked Woods Series*, Author Insight, Author Appearance, Contests and Giveaways?

Join the Wicked Woods Official Facebook Fan Page at:

http://www.facebook.com/pages/Wicked-Woods/176069965742555?v=app_4949752878

Talk to Kailin Gow, the bestselling author of over 68 distinct books for all ages at:

http://kailingow.wordpress.com

and

on Twitter at: @kailingow